LOST AND FOUND WILDERNESS

written and illustrated by
JANET HOGAN

Published by Lost Books Publishing

ISBN 978-1-961281-01-1 (hardback)

ISBN: 978-1-961281-02-8 (paperback)

Cover art and Illustrations by Janet Hogan

Book Layout and Design by Christopher Hogan, Lost Books Publishing

COPYRIGHT

Contents

My Inspiration

Recently, I had the privilege of camping in the Big Bend National Park with my youngest son and his wife. We hiked by day and listened to audio stories in their tent by night. I don't know if it was inspiration from the fantastical stories or the knowledge that I had been teaching preadolescents for 20 years, but when Emma issued a challenge out of the blue, "Janet, you should write a children's book" and Matthew supported the idea, I came home and started writing. When I was finished, my husband, Chris, told me that if I sketched out a couple of pictures and a cover design, he'd get this story out there, so here we are! I found inspiration in the unique wilderness there in Texas and in many of the people I love, bits of whom are sprinkled throughout the story. It was a fun process for me and, I hope, an enjoyable read for you.

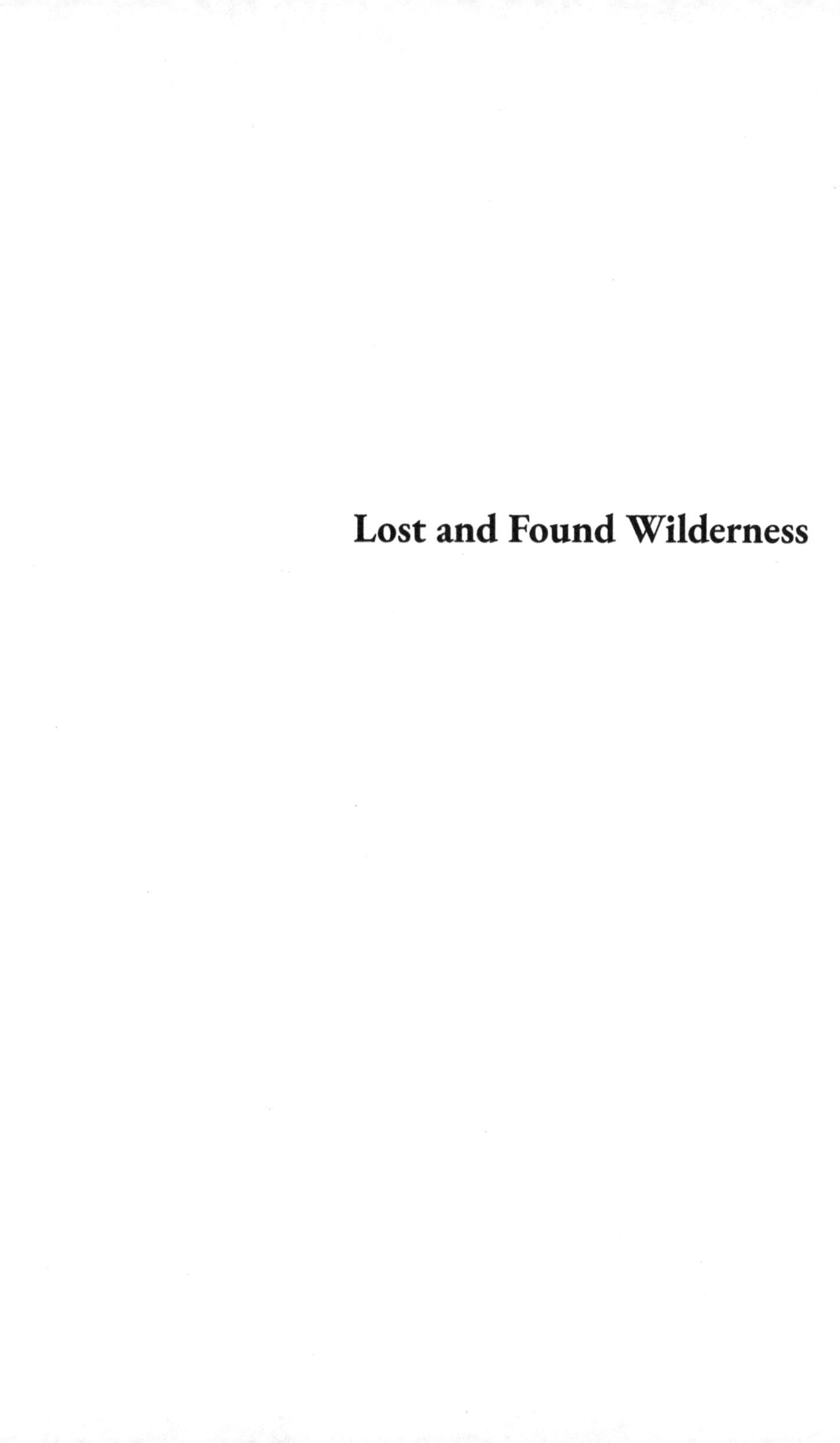

Lost and Found Wilderness

CHAPTER 1

NO OTHER CHOICE

Franklin's eyes were beginning to open but only in squinted slits, letting in a beam of fuzzy light making its way through the patches of deep green above him. He had a throbbing headache. Forcing his eyes open as much as he dared, the forest canopy slowly came into focus. He turned his aching head only to realize that he was on his back in a cushion of soggy leaves and his sister was sitting on the ground beside him.

"Are you okay?" she asked.

He was so stunned by the situation surrounding him that it took a moment for him to answer. "Lena, where are we?"

She looked down into the worried eyes that were surrounded by brown, tousled waves of hair and reached to hold onto his arm, connecting herself to her brother. He was the twin she felt so close to, even if she'd often argued with him and had a bad habit of stealing bites of his snacks. In fact, they often seemed to read each other's thoughts and once had the same dream on the same night. Right now, she wished she could read his mind and make sure he was all right after having been unconscious for hours through the night.

Lena was sure she hadn't slept a wink but had stood guard next to her helpless brother in a frightening and unfamiliar place, but her memory was clear. Their parents had been killed two days before in a horrible car wreck, so they were staying with the only person that they knew who was like family--Miss Carol. She was the kind, older, white-haired neighbor who'd watched them on rare occasions when their parents had to be away.

Mom was an only child, which meant no aunts, no uncles, and no cousins on her side. In fact, they had no aunts, uncles, or cousins at all because their dad's only brother, Uncle Benjamin, had had a fight with their dad years ago and the brothers hadn't spoken since.

The twins had no memory of him because they were told that the last time he visited was when they were babies. Oh, how the twins envied friends who had cousins and would tell about adventures with them after weekends and holidays. Having a cousin seemed like the greatest part of a family to the twins, automatic friends that would always be there your entire life.

Three of their grandparents had already passed and the one still living, their mother's mother, whom they called Grandma Judy, had to live in a special home because she had lost her memory and couldn't care for herself.

As Franklin's vision cleared and his thoughts began to order themselves, Lena spoke. "Do you remember us leaving Miss Carol's?"

"Yeah," Franklin answered. "And I remember that creepy man who gave us a ride."

After they had received the devastating news of their parents' death, the two had determined they would run away together. It seemed to be their only option since they didn't know any family and had no idea where their Uncle Benjamin lived or how to contact him. Besides, he was probably a terrible person if he didn't like their dad.

They had seen too many movies. You know - the ones with orphans being adopted by evil, abusive parents? They had also reminded each other that most people like to adopt cute babies. Now that they were about to turn eleven and there were two of them, they had decided on a bold course of action since the last thing they could imagine was being separated.

The plan was to run away and find rides with nice families until they could get to Pennsylvania and live with the Amish people they had read about. Their school lesson had left them convinced that this community, who lived a simple lifestyle, would be a comfortable and welcoming place to show up and join. They remembered that these people had nothing fancy, didn't use electricity, and didn't own cars, but rode horses, and that seemed pretty nice at the moment. Since it was May, they had talked about just attending an Amish school the last couple of weeks they had left to finish out the school year. No problem.

Lena continued the shared recollection, shaking her head with a tight grimace. "Yeah, that man seemed nice at first."

They had walked from Miss Carol's, who was probably panicking at this point, about three miles in the dark, along the one road they both remembered that led out of town. They knew that they were breaking every rule their parents had made by leaving the safety of the grown up in charge of them, but they were now following desperation and whatever they could agree on.

The new rules they'd made for themselves contained what they had learned from their mom and dad but had been adjusted to fit their new circumstances. They were only going to accept rides from women or families until they were able to safely hitchhike to Amish country. They would thank the drivers and be very polite, but would lie about their names if anyone asked, so that they wouldn't be able to be tracked later.

When they were well beyond the streetlights of town and some of the reality of what they were doing began to set in, Lena realized, "Miss Carol may call the police!"

"I was just thinking she would either do that or have the neighbors all driving around looking for us," responded Franklin.

These thoughts made their hearts race and then, they had started ducking behind bushes on the roadside when cars came by, fearing they would be discovered and taken back home and then Lord knows where.

After about half an hour of headlight dodging, Franklin finally made a declaration, "We are never going to get rides to Pennsylvania like this. We're going to have to trust someone soon and take a ride until we're far enough from home that nobody will recognize us."

Not long after Lena agreed, a white, mid-sized sedan pulled up beside them. The passenger side window rolled down revealing a soft, portly, middle-aged man who asked if they were all right.

Lena had spoken up with an awkwardly contrived lie she was inventing as she went. "We have to meet our grandparents at a restaurant down the road because our parents' car broke down."

Warning instincts in them arose, especially considering what their parents had taught them about never accepting rides from strangers, but neither sibling was in their right mind as they dealt with grief, fear, and desperation at the same time. All it took was his harmless look at just the right time and they clambered into his car, Lena in the front and Franklin in the back.

At first, all three of them sat in silence, driving out beyond their town and into the darkening mountains. Lena noticed the man's white dress shirt was drawn in by the seat belt, squeezing his soft belly in the middle, which reminded her of a giant marshmallow. His dated tie dangled over the edge of the pilloviness. He finally spoke, telling them his name was Floyd and they could call him Uncle Floyd. Then, he began quizzing them about what had happened with their parents' car and about the restaurant's location. Neither twin could give a satisfactory answer since they had not coordinated their story beforehand, and Lena hadn't thought through the details enough for it to make much sense.

Between Floyd's eerie smile and them not being too convincing with their lie, things began to get very tense. Franklin supposed it was a gentlemanly instinct that had caused him to open the door for Lena so she could get in the front seat, but then he began to regret it. It seemed like an eternity of driving further and further from home and into a more and more remote forest. Franklin had watched a familiar ski area pass by miles ago and they began to grow more and more uneasy. This seemed to be a long, dark ride with no destination.

Franklin was beginning to feel increasingly protective of his sister in the front seat, but was afraid to say anything, not knowing what Floyd's reaction would be, if that was even his real name. Their parents had told them both, when they were younger, that if an adult ever said or did anything that gave them a weird feeling in the pit of their stomach, no matter who they were, get away and do it fast. Franklin realized this was the weird feeling they were talking about.

Lena turned her head and looked over her shoulder at her brother with a tense, questioning expression and when the hair began to rise on the back of Franklin's neck, he finally knew he had to do something. When the man reached over and patted Lena's leg saying, "You're a very pretty girl," Franklin almost jumped out of his skin.

Franklin had always had a hard time speaking up for himself and other people, so he hesitated, waiting for the perfect moment or to build up enough courage, but meanwhile, his heart was pounding. He was sitting up straight, leaning forward, and breathing heavily. People always said Franklin was nice, but he thought it was mostly because he just didn't want to upset anyone, so he usually went along with what other people wanted to do or agreed with what they thought. He hated that about himself at that moment.

While panic was rising in his chest, he saw something out the window to his right. He had no idea what it was, but a strange twinkle of light at the edge of the tree line, for some reason, shook him into action. He opened his mouth to finally say something, but before any words came out,

Lena's acting instincts had taken over. Second nature from her drama team practice, they were now kicking in and she suddenly yelled, "I'm gonna be sick! Pull over!" The man had resisted at first, but she was demanding, throwing in gagging gestures, "I'm going to throw up! Stop the car!"

The man, looking confused and frazzled, finally pulled over and Lena jumped out, screaming "Run, Franklin!" He had immediately taken the cue, had joined her on the side of the road and the two of them had sprinted toward the dense forest edge where there were no streetlights and very little moonlight.

"Hey! Come back! Come back! It's dangerous out there! What are you doing?" Floyd shouted, but with only a view of their backs flying as fast as their legs could carry them, and him being in no running condition, he soon gave up with a gritty yell, "Ha! Go ahead! You'll be bear food and no one will even know you're gone!"

Neither had looked back at first, but the next thing they remembered hearing was his tires spitting gravel and then they turned to see the glow of taillights rounding the top of a hill and fading into the distance.

Their heartbeats slowly calmed, and they caught their breath in time to realize they were now in a very serious predicament. No one knew where they were, not even them, and they had no idea what to do.

Chapter 2

Into The Deep

In the fading moonlight, it grew so dark that it was hard to see where to step. They had run quite a distance into the woods and sat on the cool ground for a while to consider their options. Franklin asked, "Did you see that light right before we jumped out?"

Lena looked in his direction, "Light?"

"Yeah, some kind of sparkling light in the trees."

"No, what do you think it was?" she questioned.

"No idea," he said, "but I don't see it anymore."

Lena was inspecting a rip about four inches long in the leg of her purple pants from when she had scraped past some underbrush. Her mind went to the recent shopping trip where her mother had bought them for her. She always loved shopping with her mom. They would always buy something fun and then get a smoothie at their favorite little shop with berries painted on the walls. She sat quietly for a while, feeling the torn fabric and remembering. Franklin's next words were,

"Should we try to find the road again and hope for a good person to give us a ride?" After a little deliberation, they agreed that the risk was too high that Floyd would return. He would probably expect them to seek out the road again after they were good and scared.

It seemed like it was midnight, although they were not sure. Neither one had a watch, and they hadn't packed much but the last bottle of juice they found in the fridge and two peanut butter sandwiches they had managed to throw together in Miss Carol's kitchen. They thought luggage would draw too much attention to them so Franklin had put what they had in a small backpack, which had gotten smashed flat when he had fallen on it.

Their desperation had given them the energy to forget their tired legs and to trek what seemed like four or five miles into the forest, looking for another road or some sign of civilization. In the thin slice of moonlight they had, Lena had begun to barely see the ground drop off and managed to dodge it, but Franklin hadn't noticed the ravine, had stepped into it, lost his balance, and had fallen quite a distance. Lena was left terrified in the thick darkness and only able to hear his helpless gasps and the tumbling sounds that ended in a thud. When he hadn't responded to her calls, she felt her way through the brush and down the slope on her hands and knees until she finally found her brother lying on his back as still as death. She leaned over his face until she felt his breath and, then, listened for a heartbeat. Only when her ear felt the rhythmic thump, tha-thump, tha-thump did she take a relieved breath.

Settling in for what would be a sleepless night, she could only make out, by the shred of moonlight, edges of the ravine with long, dark tree roots grasping at the sandy slope's edges like long, dark, boney witch's fingers holding up a wall and it left her with an eerie chill. She was glad Franklin had insisted on them bringing light jackets because she could feel the temperature dropping as the night continued. She pulled his jacket out of the backpack and covered him with it like a blanket, then untied the arms of hers from around her waist and slipped it on.

She stood guard for hours, waiting for a response from her brother and was wide awake to watch the morning sun slowly rise. The forest gradually brightened, and Franklin finally began to stir. Lena was so relieved! Instead of being tempted to tease him or thump him on his sore head like she might normally do, all she wanted was to hug him and shout for joy! She knew he was all right as he recalled all the night's events with her, and then he took charge. Franklin suddenly stood up and insisted that his head was fine and that they should continue walking in the same direction they had been heading. She didn't bother to mention that she had noticed a bump on the left side of his skull as she held his head through the night.

Lena had heard of concussions but didn't know how to diagnose one or what to do about it, so she opted to stay silent. All she really knew was that they were, basically, a brain bruise you could get if you hit your head really hard and one symptom was unevenly dilated pupils of your eyes. Her clever move was to ask him to check her eye for a loose eyelash so that she could peer into his eyes looking for matching black centers without explaining what she was doing. She didn't want to worry her brother. They looked even to her in the morning light, so she never brought up her concern.

Franklin didn't know if it was because he was two minutes older and slightly taller, but he had the sense that it was his duty to protect his sister and he began leading the way through what seemed like miles of forest and into a space that opened up wide. It was an enormous valley of open grassy fields with rounded mounds of mountains surrounding them.

To their far left, they spotted a stream of water and immediately made their way to it since they had shared their juice bottle hours before and were getting thirsty.

"That smashed sandwich looked disgusting at first, but it wasn't too bad. I wish we had five more right now," Franklin commented as they picked up their stride toward the water.

Both had washed down the smashed sandwich they split and planned to save the other for later. They had kept the empty juice bottle for two reasons: there were no garbage cans and they both hated litter, plus, they thought they should save it to refill when they found water, and here it was!

Nearing the rushing water made them realize how thirsty they were, and they both began to run with strength they didn't know they had. It was the prettiest little steam they had ever seen, meandering through the rolling land, tumbling over worn, weathered rocks, and edged with several colors of wildflowers.

As soon as they stuck their hands into the cool liquid, Lena had a sudden hesitation, "Wait. Should we drink this stuff? Dirt, bugs, roots....ewwww!"

Then she and Franklin remembered together their dad explaining to them how the rocks actually purify the water if it's moving over them fast enough. They relaxed, comforted by this shared memory, and buried their faces in the flow, slurping and laughing at themselves and each other. Once they drank all they could hold, they filled their bottle and decided to follow the stream as they moved forward.

"You never know how long it will take us to get out of here and we might get thirsty again," decided Franklin.

They walked a couple more miles and Lena started feeling the exhaustion she had been ignoring. They were both feeling thankful their parents had hiked often with them, which had built up their walking stamina, but she was pretty certain she had not slept a wink all night while she sat by her brother, waiting for him to wake up.

"Franklin, don't be mad at me, but I can't walk another step. Can we please take another break?"

Her brother had mixed feelings at this point. Part of him was sorry she was so worn out and he appreciated her watching over him all night, but part of him was worried that they wouldn't reach civilization before the sun went down if they kept stopping. "Just a little further," he coaxed.

"I'll try," Lena answered.

They didn't make it very far before Lena tripped on a rock and fell to her knees. Franklin reached for her hand to pull her up, but she suddenly burst into tears. And then, sobs. Many feelings hit her at once and she cried out, "Franklin! Mom and Dad are gone!"

As she heaved and shook, it made him choke up. He sat beside her and put his hand softly on her back. Then he felt a warm sensation move through his body and to his chest. It got stuck there for a moment and almost hurt, but finally made its way to his throat and then released itself through his eyes in warm tears.

They had been so stunned and scared by the initial news of what had happened to their parents that they had not stopped to completely realize the sadness of it all. Franklin's mind had gone into problem-solving mode and Lena's into panic. It had kept the sadness buried way down in her belly. The two of them sat together silently for almost an hour when they finally released their hug and were able to speak again.

They continued the walk, which was getting slower and slower on exhausted legs, but they were amazed by the scenery surrounding them. The clear meadows looked like paintings with the deep red, purple and yellow wildflowers sprinkled into the lush green grasses. They decided that they lived in the best place in the world. Most people would think this picture was fiction and they had these very same flowers near their home - at least their past home. Lena didn't know all the flowers by name, but called out the ones she could identify as they walked past. Monkeyflower, Paintbrushes, Columbine, and Dwarf Sunflowers, which were her favorites.

It wasn't too much longer when they noticed that the sun was much lower in the sky than they had remembered. When she realized how late it was getting, Lena plopped into the scratchy golden grass and started shaking her head back and forth. "It's going to get dark again before long and we have no idea where we are or where we're going!" Then she let out a scream that seemed to boil up from her toes and it rattled the air around them.

To Franklin, she sounded like a wild animal caught in a trap. It scared him to see his sister so helpless and terrified, but giving in to the thoughts of what could happen to them was not an option. The scream stopped after all the air was out of her lungs and she looked tired, but fine.

He made a quick decision and reached for her arm, pulling her to her feet. "Sis, we can NOT give up. Do you hear me? If we want to be rescued, we're going to have to keep going till we find people! Besides, Mom and Dad would expect us to be strong."

Just as Lena was steadying her tired legs, they both heard an unusual noise. It was high-pitched and seemed out of place in their surroundings. Lena looked at her brother and asked, "Did you hear that?"

Franklin nodded yes.

"It almost sounded like someone was watching a cartoon in another room," she added.

"But, that doesn't make sense," he replied. "We can't both be having the same hallucination," Franklin chuckled, but with a slightly concerned expression on his face. They stood frozen for a moment, waiting to hear more, but nothing came.

After a few tugs, Lena gave in and started walking beside her brother again, hanging onto his arm this time, still following the stream. He was a little taller than her, and stronger. His soccer playing had given him muscular legs and plenty of stamina and leaning on his strength was giving her a little comfort. She imagined him as her big brother at that moment, even though he was only two minutes older.

When she looked ahead, she could see that their open field was coming to an end, and they were heading back toward more dense forest. The trees all looked like Christmas trees to Franklin. He thought of these firs and pines that way all year long because of how he and his dad would always find a perfect one in the summertime, mark it, and let it grow a little more before cutting it down and dragging it to their house after Thanksgiving dinner.

But the forest might as well have been a haunted house to Lena. She didn't say anything just yet, and didn't turn her head much, but gave a side glance at Franklin's face to try and read his reaction to what was coming.

He, clearly, could see what was ahead, but he wasn't saying a word and not slowing down. With his face fixed on the path forward, they trudged in silence for at least half an hour. As they got closer, it seemed as if the branches of the oak and aspen trees, sprinkled in among the evergreens, were waving them into the deep and Lena felt a shiver go up her spine.

Finally, she broke the silence. "Are we, seriously, going there?"

Franklin's quick and strong response was, "We have no choice." Inside, he was feeling shaky and unsure, but he didn't want to let Lena know that. He had decided to be in charge - at least for now.

Chapter 3

Unexplainable

"Do you notice how the sun is setting at the exact moment we're reaching the edge of the trees?" Franklin asked as they closed in on the woods' edge.

"Yes! Almost like we're in a play and stage directors are planning this!" Lena answered with raised eyebrows.

And then they had a "twin moment," as they called it. They both looked through the sides of their eyes at each other and said, at the exact same time, "So weird..."

For some reason, the fear that had been stalking Lena was disappearing and Franklin's determination to find civilization was rising. They walked and rested, walked and rested for another two hours in darkness that was filled with eerie sounds and a damp chill. The only guide they had was the little beam of light from the moon that cast a subtle shimmer on the stream that was now growing narrow. Neither of them could believe how far they had trekked, but they knew some unusual kind of energy was propelling them.

As Lena's mind calmed, she noticed things she hadn't before. Even though it was hard to feel it, she knew they had been walking uphill. "Franklin, can you tell we're climbing?"

"I can't tell if we are or not. How do you know?" he asked.

Both were good students, but Lena loved science, especially, and she had a reputation for pulling out some random piece of scientific information from her back pocket when you least expected it. She had been watching the movement of the stream's water by the moonlight. "The stream is flowing opposite of the way we're walking, and rivers and streams always flow downhill," came her confident reply.

"Always?" he quizzed.

"Well, they are pulled downhill by gravity, like they're pouring, birdbrain. They don't run on a motor!"

Franklin chuckled. The old Lena was returning.

They sat down for a brief rest and to eat their final sandwich. The two of them were so hungry they couldn't save it till the next day like they had planned. Both were filled with hope that they would be rescued soon, and they agreed that they needed it more now than they would later. Franklin pulled it out of his backpack, carefully tore it into two pieces, and they ate slowly, savoring each smashed bite. Peanut butter had never tasted so good. Once the last bite was swallowed and washed down with the water from their bottle, they stood up to continue on.

About five minutes later, however, Lena stopped. The brown loafers she was wearing were much less comfortable than Franklin's sneakers and were rubbing blisters on her feet. "I cannot go another step," she protested. She had put on the brakes and was plopping down on the cool, moss forest floor.

Franklin sat patiently beside her. "Okay, we're miles and miles away from the road we left, right?" he asked. She nodded, anxiously waiting for the solution that seemed to be coming. "That means we must be getting closer to something else. Somewhere there are people. We just can't give up."

"Great. That's the plan? What if we're in the middle of nowhere and it's even further to civilization in this direction than going back?" she replied in frustration.

"Nah, I don't think so," Franklin insisted. "There's only so much wilderness out here. If we don't find a major road, we'll find a house or......"

Just at that moment, they both noticed little lights in the distance. Lights! Not just a few, but several. The night was so black that they looked as bright as sparklers. They didn't seem as stable as the light from electric bulbs, but had a slight, familiar vibration to them. They both gasped and Lena shouted, "It's got to be a camp site! Those must be camp lanterns!! We're saved!!!!"

They jumped to their feet with energy that surprised them and with huge grins on their exhausted faces. *That was a crazy experience getting lost in the wilderness so long!* they thought simultaneously.

They stepped toward the campgrounds, trusting there would be kind people that would feed them and help them, but, just as they did, the lanterns moved. And what was really strange, is that they all moved at the same time. And then, they began to swirl around in the blackness. Tiny lights, now dipping and rising in the air. As they moved, they seemed to twinkle.

Franklin flashed back to the light he had seen when they first jumped out of the car. Was this connected...?

Lena and Franklin shook their heads. What was happening? The lights they thought were larger and off in the distance now looked much closer and very small. And then it dawned on Franklin. "Those aren't lanterns. They're fireflies."

"Do you mean they're lightning bugs?"

"Yep."

The two of them stood there in awe for a long moment. They felt extreme disappointment and a sense of wonder at the same time. Lena felt Franklin's arm rest on her shoulder. And then, while they stared in disbelief, the fireflies, now appearing by the thousands, formed a shape that began to undulate and flow in a pattern that appeared to be trying to direct them.

They turned to each other at the same time while Lena asked, choking out her words very slowly, “Are...they...trying...to...get...us...to...go...over...there?” pointing to their right and away from the stream.

“That’s the craziest thing I ever heard, but I was thinking the same thing,” Franklin replied while squeezing her arm.

After a few deep breaths, Lena prodded, “Should we try?”

“Well, what have we got to lose?” Franklin shrugged.

They held onto each other now and, stepping hesitantly, at first, toward the glow, they saw the formation move as they moved, keeping a consistent distance, but directing them slowly, a little further into the woods. Lena searched her memory for what she had read about lightning bugs. She recalled that they were a type of beetle. Chemicals mixing in their abdomens caused a reaction which created their bioluminescent glow. Many species were endangered, but she never remembered reading anything about them behaving like this.

The twins’ senses were heightened now, and they became aware of sounds they had mostly ignored the night before. Details were becoming distinct-- owl hoots in the distance, cricket clatter all around them, a choir of croaking frogs, the sound of the rushing water becoming softer as they moved farther and farther from it. Their sense of the situation slowly turned from eerie into magical as they accepted the guidance of what seemed almost like little forest fairies. They began to pick up the pace as an unexplainable trust took over and, as they did, the fireflies sped up, too.

Lena whispered, almost in reverence, "This is so crazy and yet, so amazing."

After a time of follow-the-leader, they came to a small clearing in the middle of all the dense trees. A large pile of soft leaves and tree needles were in the center, and it was at that point that the fireflies stopped. They formed a straight line that hovered in the black air and then whipped around the trees so quickly that there was no option of following them, and then they were gone.

It seemed clear to Franklin and Lena that this was the end of the line. The place they had been directed to. "What are we supposed to do now?" questioned Lena.

"Maybe rest?" Franklin yawned somewhat hesitantly.

It felt to Lena like they were in the middle of their own fairytale, and she began to prod her brother. "Those were no ordinary fireflies. Do you remember when we heard those strange noises that sounded like a cartoon or something? What was that and what's going on out here?"

Franklin didn't answer. They stood in the darkness stunned and exhausted.

After lingering for a moment in the middle of the cricket chorus, an intoxicating sleepiness hit them. Though they didn't say another word, they shared a knowing that they were somehow safe, somehow watched over. First, Lena sat down in the leaf pile. Then, Franklin joined her. They slowly dug their legs and then their bellies into the warm decaying forest floor that wrapped them like a blanket and allowed them to fall into the deep, healing sleep they both so desperately needed.

CHAPTER 4

AM I DREAMING?

In his next conscious moment Franklin felt something brush softly across his hand. This stirred him awake just enough to crack his eyes and realize the night had passed. Sunbeams were, again, streaming through a dense canopy of forest green and sending soft, filtered light through the trees. This time, he had no headache, only intense curiosity.

He heard a rustling beside his head, but before he could turn to see what it was he heard words. High-pitched, quick words, "You must be hungry." The voice was small and staccato. Cute. He turned his neck to see a chipmunk about three feet to his right who seemed to have no fear of humans. He just sat there staring at Franklin who was frozen for fear of scaring off the little visitor.

He slowly reached over, elbowed Lena, and whispered through the side of his mouth. "Wake up. We have a cute little chipmunk stalking us." As Lena was stirring, the voice came again.

"My name is Mitchie. Don't worry. We're going to take care of you."

"Wait a second..." Franklin thought out loud. This makes no sense, but it suddenly dawned on Franklin that while he heard these chopped little words that he had ignored for a moment, this chipmunk's mouth was moving. And when the words stopped, its mouth stopped and only its whiskers were twitching. But, of course, that couldn't be.

By this time, he could feel Lena rising up to prop her head on an elbow, allowing her to peer stealthily over Franklin's chest to view the littlest, cutest, big-eyed chipmunk she'd ever seen. "Franklin is that chipmunk talking to us?" she whispered.

"No way, silly. I'm just trying to figure out where those words are coming from," was his shaken reply. Then it started again.

"I hear you guys think that's impossible, but you might be surprised to learn all that *is* actually possible."

There was no way he could ignore those words now, but he couldn't make his confused mind grasp what was happening. Again, the chipmunk's mouth was moving. Franklin jumped up frantically and shouted into the trees. "Okay! Who's pranking us? Who's out there?!" Only silence followed.

Lena lay there for a long, still moment while a fuzzy little brown rodent with big, soft eyes, dark racing stripes down its sides and slightly bucked teeth explained, "All animals talk. I know you can't believe it yet, but we do. We only speak to each other, though, because we need to maintain a distance from humans for our survival." The creature paused for a moment looking to see if Franklin was calming down and then, with a paw scratching its belly, continued. "Throughout time, each generation of animals tends to find one person they can trust who is either living away from civilization or who needs help and is away from all other people and then we speak with them. Almost every one of them has been trustworthy and hasn't given us away, we suppose, because there has never been a group of humans capture us, expecting to hear us speak.

"If anyone did tell, I imagine the other humans thought they were either crazy or had hallucinated from eating the wrong wild berries, chi chi chi." These last three syllables appeared to be a chuckle because the chipmunk's eyes closed, its lips curved upward, and its belly shook when it made the sounds. "You are our generation's people! We're getting two for one!"

The animal plopped backward in a trusting pose, leaning against its long, bristly tail with its little hind feet sticking straight out toward them. When the talking stopped, Lena looked up from the chipmunk to see her brother staring down at them. Both twins' mouths were hanging open. Franklin slowly lowered himself back into the leaves, still completely stunned and puzzled.

Now it was their turn to respond. Franklin had always had an unusual bond with animals. Before he was old enough to learn that veterinarians often had to do painful things to help animals, that had been his plan for a career. Whenever they had hiked through the woods at home, visited a zoo, or vacationed where animals were, he gravitated towards them and spent more time with them than family or friends. Animals had always seemed less afraid of him than other people and often looked him in the eyes. Once, a tiger at the zoo astounded the crowd by walking across the habitat and straight up to him, locked eyes with him, and stood there a long time with the Plexiglas separating their faces by only inches.

Did he have some sort of gift that the chipmunk was responding to? Could this be true? Was he dreaming? Did hitting his head make him hallucinate? While he contemplated the possibilities, Lena elbowed him.

"Mitchie? Did he say his name was Mitchie?"

"Yes! That's me!" came the clipped response. "Now, will you tell me your names?" The chipmunk rocked forward, tucking his hind feet back under himself and widening his eyes in anticipation.

Before Franklin's intellect had time to edit his response, he found himself saying, "Franklin. I'm Franklin and this is my twin sister, Lena."

"Oh! I'm so excited! You are the only humans we animals, in this forest, have ever talked with! My parents' generation didn't get a human because this doesn't happen very often, so my grandfather told me everything I know about your species! We wished and wished and now...here you are!"

Lena was slowly edging up into a sitting position next to her brother and they were wishing with all their might that the little fellow would stay and not disappear like a dream.

"We picked you some huckleberries because we knew you must be hungry!" Mitchie pointed with his little forepaw and there, on a clean pile of flattened leaves were two lumps of little purple, grape-looking fruit piled about eight inches high!

"We're starved!" shouted Franklin, now losing his timid approach.

"That looks delicious!" declared Lena as she dove into her portion, shoving berries into her mouth, chewing, smiling, juice staining her tongue, teeth and chin. She checked on their new little friend from the corner of her eyes. What she saw was a cute, chubby little chipmunk rocking backward again, squinting his eyes shut and chuckling, "Chi chi chi!"

"*We* picked?" Franklin asked with sudden curiosity.

"Yes, our community's chipmunks," Mitchie answered.

"Thank you!" the twins' grateful voices chimed in unison. As the last of the berries were being swallowed, Franklin wondered, "Where are all these other chipmunks? There had to be quite a few to do all this work."

Mitchie looked over his left shoulder and then his right and began making sounds that were high pitched in an evenly spaced rhythm that, to them, sounded just like a bird chirping. Three and four at a time, chipmunks scampered into the clearing from the tops of trees and behind their trunks. Some were giggling, some came up close, and some stopped to keep their distance.

A different chipmunk ran up and onto Franklin's leg, which startled him a bit at first. This chipmunk seemed like an adolescent, but he couldn't tell his age for sure. He was surprised at how clearly he could tell the difference between this one and Mitchie.

Franklin felt the tiny claws pricking through the fabric of his jeans, but once he got used to it, he hoped the little creature would never leave.

Pockie introduced himself and then volunteered, "We love fungi, but we didn't think you'd want to eat that - chi-chi. It looks like you like huckleberries!"

"We love them!" Lena finally responded. She had been too stunned to speak until this point.

"Yeah, thanks for sparing us the fungus!" Franklin joked. "Is there anything else around here we can eat? I don't mean for you guys to do the work. Lena and I are happy to do it. We just haven't eaten much in the last couple of days."

The chipmunks all began to look at each other and then little murmurings were heard that couldn't quite be distinguished, but it was clear they were planning to help. Franklin looked over at his sister and they shared a sparkled-eyed smile unlike any they had shared before. Contained in it were the satisfaction of sensing that their needs would somehow be met and a discovery they had never, in their wildest imaginations, thought they would make, and they were making it together.

"Thank you all!" Franklin announced, and Lena followed with, "Yes! Thank you! We were so hungry, and the berries were great!" They noticed that a hum of soft noises and head nods rippled through the crowd that surrounded them.

"Come see me." Lena patted on her leg, coaxing Pockie to visit her. He quickly complied and sat there on the rip in her pants leg looking up at her kind face with complete fascination. He stared at her long, smooth, brown hair and large, dark eyes that seemed to be smiling at him.

While she felt his warm little body vibrating on both cloth and bare skin, she admired the white stripes running down his brown sides that were bordered in black. On his face were extensions of the pattern that reminded her of war paint, but Pockie seemed more like a party boy than a fighter. His tail was as long as he was and that was about eight inches. All fear and hesitation had left her, but she resisted the urge to pick him up and squeeze him like she wanted so badly to do. Her instincts told her that might be going a little too far.

Mitchie seemed older, fully grown. Even though he was very friendly and possessed a jolly personality, he had a little reservation that seemed to always come with maturity. He stood back about a foot from the twins and observed as Pockie frolicked around in their laps and as they carefully reached out to touch him for the first time with their hands.

Hands. There was something about them, decided Mitchie. He noticed his heart rate changed when Lena reached for

Pockie's head. Legs were one thing, but hands could grab a little animal. Yet, he trusted Franklin and Lena, and as he came to this conclusion, his heartbeat began to slow.

Mitchie shook out his fur. "I know this isn't enough food to last you the whole day, so I can show you where some other food is when you're ready. Once you know where to find it and what it looks like, you can eat when you like."

Pockie pushed his head under Franklin's palm and began to rub it back and forth. "Does that feel good, little buddy?" asked Franklin.

"Sure does!" Pockie looked up at his chocolate eyes. He noticed that Lena's eyes were so dark the brown melted into her pupils, but the brown in Franklin's had a gold rim around the edges.

"I need to put you down for now so we can go with Mitchie, but I will rub your head more later," Franklin promised. He could actually see Pockie smile. It was a tiny smile, but his face lit up. Then, he scampered over to a group of chipmunks that seemed to be anxiously waiting for him.

Chapter 5

Exploring Their Wilderness

Lena hesitated but finally asked as they stood up and addressed Mitchie. "Do you really need to show us where food is if we're going to be leaving the woods today?" Franklin stiffened as he considered the answer to her question.

Mitchie waited a moment and then replied, "I'm afraid you won't be out of the woods today."

She choked at hearing this and then Franklin took over. "How far from civilization are we?"

"In terms of miles, I'm not exactly sure, but it's many. We're in the middle of a vast wilderness," Mitchie told them. "You've come a long way; probably further than you realize."

The twins looked at each other in silence. Neither said a word. They were experiencing extreme exhaustion and painful emotions, yet an excited anticipation of what could be next with these animals. These wild animals. The greater part of them felt like they were, in spite of everything, in the middle of an exciting adventure.

Mitchie broke the tension by commanding, “Let’s go! I know where there are some mushrooms we really like. I bet you’ll like them too!” Franklin & Lena took one quick look at each other and then began to follow him.

They were still in shock that they were communicating with, and now following, a rodent. The thought made them shake their heads, but somehow, they were accepting the crazy situation and had decided to just go with it.

He took them back to the stream of water first so they could drink & refill their bottle, then they proceeded about one hundred yards to a patch where some special delights were growing. Franklin guessed at the distance because their trip seemed to be about the length of a football field. There, all over the ground, were little yellowish-brown growths that looked like sponges - the natural sea-animal type.

Lena asked, “Are these morel mushrooms?”

“Yes, they are! Very good!” answered Mitchie. “Are you a plant expert or something?”

Franklin rolled his eyes. "She knows a lot about anything related to science." He followed his sarcastic tone with a smile that always made Lena feel satisfied.

She loved knowing a lot of facts. She knew it impressed her brother, and the facts often came in handy.

Mitchie said, "I guess you already know the difference between these and the poisonous ones then, I hope."

"I think so, but maybe you should show us just to be safe," came her wise response.

Mitchie promised to point out the first inedibles they found and after plucking a shirttail full of the morels from the ground, they hiked on. As they were making their way toward a ravine, Franklin adjusted his grip on the bottom of his mushroom-filled shirt and asked Mitchie what he liked to eat.

Mitchie immediately responded, "These!" pointing to the loaded shirt.

"Well, you have good taste," Lena agreed. "Morels are expensive for humans. I read that chefs love to cook with them, but Franklin and I have never eaten any before. I'm kind of excited to try them."

Mitchie continued, "We also like flowers, worms, berries, insects, other fungi, grasses, seeds...... We're not very picky, really." After thinking another minute, he said, "You know .....there are three different types of trout in that stream if we could just figure out how to catch them for you...but, for now, I have more plants to show you!"

As the day continued, Mitchie showed them where to find wild asparagus, though they had to dig through tangled bramble to get the little spears, wild strawberries, which were delicious, but tiny so it took a lot of work to pick much volume, dandelions, plums, orache, which are little salty, green, leafy plants, prickly pear cactus, and how to recognize the poisonous plants.

Each time they found something new, Mitchie told them about the nutrients in them and which parts to eat if they weren't sure. They snacked along the way, and they decided all of them were pretty good, though Franklin wasn't sure about the flavor of the orache. Besides, it reminded him of little clover leaves and took hundreds to be enough to make a human-sized salad. The dandelion leaves were more his style.

When Lena was about to climb a plum tree and toss down some sweet fruit, the three of them looked out into a space to their left and saw a herd of beefy, shaggy deer. While Mitchie reminded the twins that they were elk, the largest one approached the tree in a slow, but confident stride.

Franklin felt his body tighten a bit as he remembered his dad telling them that hunters had to be careful not to get impaled by the antlers of a protective bull elk. Just at the moment he had that thought, the elk lowered his head and said, “Mitchie, I see you’ve found the humans.”

“Yes! These are Franklin and Lena. They were lost and alone.

The massive elk came closer and a deep, husky voice declared, “My name is Buck. If you need anything, just let us know. Our females are giving birth now and there may be extra milk if you need some.”

“Whoa!” thought Lena and Franklin at the same time. “Elk milk?” While they considered the strange offer, they looked out to the mama cows and saw several little calves teetering on wobbly legs that seemed to barely hold them up. It made them look so cute and helpless. But while they were busy being amazed by the whole scene, Mitchie had the presence of mind to thank Buck who was retracing steps back to his herd.

Lena realized she had expected all the animals to know each other and was surprised by this unfamiliar encounter but could tell Mitchie didn't know Buck. Maybe it was because they were wandering a little further from home than Mitchie usually traveled. She had more questions than she was comfortable asking. She finally shouted a thank you to the huge and intimidating, but kind bull elk. That prompted Franklin to wave to the herd, which he later decided was pretty dumb, but all the cows had looked up and seemed to smile at them. At least that's what they swore to each other later that they had seen.

On their way back to the clearing where they had begun their day, to drop off the last of their groceries, Mitchie directed them to some water for a drink. When they got close, Lena noticed right away that the water wasn't flowing. It was as still as the rocks scattered in it. This made her hesitate because she knew that the chances of microscopic organisms living in it were high and those could make them sick. Just as Franklin was mumbling something about germs, she saw a few glossy, black beetles that she recognized. They were huge - over an inch long. Franklin was telling Mitchie that he appreciated the help, but animals could drink things humans couldn't. He knew their stomachs were different somehow.

Lena interrupted their conversation. "Franklin! Look! Scavenger Beetles! That's a good sign! He walked over to her pointing finger and saw the black, domed insects with V-shaped hind legs in the water and asked, "What do you mean?" "See that leaf floating with a bunch of tiny eggs on it? And these little brown worm-looking things?" "Yeah" he responded. "Those are the eggs of these beetles, and the brown things are larvae, I think." She paused and squinted. "But they live in this water, so I think it's a good sign that the water's safe to drink. And look! See! snails too!"

"What makes you think bugs in water is a good sign?" Franklin asked with a snicker.

"Well, I think it's kinda like the more creatures we *can* see, the less creatures we *can't* see. Like the ones we see eat the microscopic ones."

Franklin gave her a long look, rolled his eyes, shook his head, and asked, "Well, are you going to be the one to sample it?"

"I guess so, if my big brother's too scared," Lena smirked. "I guess somebody's got to be the guinea pig."

Franklin noticed his sister's sarcasm was returning which, for her, was a good sign. He smiled to himself and watched her lean over and fill their bottle in what looked like a pond connected to a stream at the far side. She took a sip and pronounced herself "not dead," so they walked on.

By this time, the sun was beginning to set and as they walked back, they realized they would definitely be spending another night in the forest. A combination of worry and excitement settled over them. The experiences they were having would have been unimaginable a few days before, but they didn't want to think about the future too much or the fact that people would certainly be looking for them by now.

When they reached the clearing they had started from, they found a literal crowd of chipmunks lined up and waiting for them. There were mother chipmunks herding their litters of five to eight youngsters each, and father chipmunks who must have been working very hard because the food the twins hadn't eaten along the way had been stacked and organized and their leaf pile bed was larger than before, had been fluffed, and was looking very inviting.

With moonlight beginning to fill the sky as it traded places with the orange, setting sun, the twins sat on the ground near their pile of leaves and thanked all of their special helpers. They went around the ring that encircled them asking for every name, trying their best to remember them. They felt their hearts melting as they watched the mother chipmunks with their tiny little furry babies frolicking around them or drinking their milk. They were happy to see Pockie run up to them as the last name was being called out. Without hesitation again, he began to run up their legs and settle in their laps for a rub.

Franklin was relieved to realize he immediately recognized Pockie among all the others. Even though he had a special way with animals, he had worried that all the chipmunks might look alike to him. It was becoming important to be able to distinguish between these animals as he realized their personalities differed as much as humans do.

There was just something about Pockie: his trusting nature, his playfulness, his curiosity, and his immediate affection for the two humans. Franklin decided that any personality that trusting must be trustworthy himself and this thought warmed his heart when Pockie snuggled up under his hand again and peered out from under Franklin's fingers to smile up into his eyes.

The siblings ate some more from their food stash, polished off their water, put on their jackets as the temperature dropped off, and stayed up late into the night as the other animals disappeared little by little until Pockie was the only one left. They played with him until they were completely exhausted.

Climbing into their leafy bed, Franklin's mind was filled with images of all the creatures he had spent time with that day and how much he wished he could draw or paint them. He was sure Lena would be wishing for a camera, but he could hold onto special moments best by drawing them.

Franklin had decided art was his true talent. He was pretty good at sports, but he got a lot of compliments at school and from his family every time he would draw, and most of the time, his drawings were of animals. If he couldn't be a veterinarian, at least he could capture some of his favorite things with a pencil or paint. He wished so badly he had brought a pencil and his sketch pad to try to record parts of this unbelievable day.

Just before their eyelids got too heavy, Lena asked Franklin if this would be their home for a while and what would they do if it rained. He was quiet for a long time with his eyes shut and she thought he must have fallen asleep, but he finally murmured, "We'll worry about that tomorrow."

Chapter 6

Leave or Stay?

The warmth of the morning sun streaked across Lena's face. She rubbed her eyes and propped up on one elbow. "Well, I guess it hasn't been a dream."

Franklin rolled over to face his sister. "Yeah, here we are, and... ANIMALS CAN TALK!" After a brief pause and with his eyes squinted, he added, "That did happen, right?"

"Yes!" she confirmed. "Let's see where they are!"

They hopped up looking for their new friends, but it took a while for them to start popping into view. Just as the twins began to doubt their magical experience, Mitchie was the first to appear.

"Well, hello, sleepy heads!" he greeted.

"What? What time is it?" asked Franklin.

"I have no idea what you call it. We don't have clocks, but we've been up a long time doing our usual routines of foraging, checking our nests, eating, and playing.

"Well, we still consider it morning." Lena smiled as she tried guessing the time based on the sun's position in the sky.

"Hmm, that's East since the sun is over there, and..."

Mitchie interrupted. "No, that's West."

Lena countered, "But if it rises in the east and sets in the west, how can..." Lena's mind frequently buzzing with science facts, knew the sun doesn't literally rise and set; it just looks like it since the Earth rotates, but she knew she'd annoy her brother if she said what she was thinking, so she resisted.

Now Franklin was interrupting. "If the sun is in the West, what does that mean?"

Mitchie answered, "You guys have been asleep longer than you think. You must be exhausted! I told the gang to leave you alone. I had to fuss a little at Pockie because he wanted to wake you up so badly," and then Mitchie seemed to wink.

Wink! Who would ever imagine a chipmunk winking, they wondered as they smiled at each other. It seemed to be the wink of a wise, patient, and more mature personality who understood more than they realized.

"Heeeeeeeeey!!" A squeal came from around a tree trunk. It was Pockie just joining the three who were now taking a seat on the ground. He didn't make another noise, but jumped right between Franklin and Lena, ran up Franklin's leg and onto his lap. After he got a few pats and greetings from Franklin, he scampered over to Lena for more attention. They were noticing that while Mitchie kept a bit of a distance, spoke often, and played the role of their guide, Pockie said very little, but wanted to be in their physical presence whenever possible. The twins' deep affection for them both was growing, and they seemed to appreciate their differences. Both chipmunks had a special role to play in their new lives.

While the animals went about their afternoon, Franklin and Lena walked around the area talking about what to do next. Their options, they decided, were to either strike out again in the direction they had been going or stay another night in the little clearing. Not knowing what was ahead made them nervous about leaving and, with the sun already sinking down into the western sky, they concluded they should stay. Besides, they couldn't imagine leaving these animals behind. Franklin suggested they search for a place to get cover in case of rain even though the skies looked sunny and blue, so they struck out on a walk.

They were alone again and not sure where Mitchie had gone, but they found a tall Douglas fir tree with an unusual shape and decided it would be their marker. It was taller than the ones around it and Franklin pointed out that if they just kept sight of that tree, they could find the way back to their current spot, which didn't seem too far from the clearing.

As they wandered, they noticed familiar plants that Mitchie had taught them were safe to eat and they began snacking on them to keep from getting too hungry. They couldn't make it out completely through the dense trees, but in the far distance, they saw where the woods opened up into a meadow and they thought they saw the ground rise up into a tall hill or cliff of some kind.

Stepping a little closer, they saw that it was something they definitely wanted to check out. If there was an overhang, it might be deep enough to stay under during the rain. They didn't have extra clothes to change into if they got soaked so they agreed it was a smart idea to be prepared.

While they talked about the possibilities, they both realized that they were planning as if they would be staying a while. Lena was the first to say it. "Do we really want to leave here?"

Franklin was quiet for a while as they walked on, but then answered, "It would be like leaving the magic. Would we ever hear animals talk again? Probably not."

This caused an immediate response from Lena. “We have to stay!”

“There’s so much we don’t know about surviving here, though, Lena,” said Franklin. “What if there are dangerous animals and what if we run out of wild food out here?”

By that time, they were finally close enough to discover that what they had seen was the side of a mountain. They were at the base of a fairly large one and its ledges to their right were covered with mountain goats. They were amazed to see the surefooted climbers zigzagging back and forth up cliffs that looked almost completely vertical.

After being entertained for some time by the steadiness and balance of these astonishing creatures, Lena looked up toward the top of the mountain and saw a couple of longhorn sheep. While she was pointing them out, Franklin remembered to check over his shoulder for their tree. The one they would go back to. The one that wasn’t... exactly where he thought it was. He panned back and forth slowly and then spoke. “Lena, the tree is right over there, right?” He pointed to a sea of deep green. All of the trees suddenly looked identical.

“Uh oh,” was all she said.

They decided to walk back in the direction they thought they had come from. Both agreed about the general direction at first, but after walking for about five minutes, they were remembering coming from different angles. They also noticed that the sun was about to set.

This new fear that was becoming familiar began to set in and Lena grabbed Franklin's arm and let off a little steam. "I thought you knew where the tree was! That was your idea!"

"I know. I thought I knew exactly where it was, but..." Then it occurred to Franklin that things were different this time. They had a new advantage. "Mitchie! Mitchie! Can you hear me?"

Immediately Lena felt relief hearing him call out to their new friend. It made her remember too, that everything was different now. He called out a couple of times, but no answer came, so they kept walking.

Lena tried, "Mit - chieeeee!"

No sooner had she gotten the last syllable out than they heard a little skittering at their feet and that adorable little clipped voice huffing and puffing, "Sorry! I was looking for something! You guys took off quicker than I realized!"

Franklin spoke up, “I’m sorry, Mitchie. We didn’t mean to worry you. We were checking out that mountain for a place to stay if it rains.”

Mitchie seemed to ignore his concern, but looked back and forth and said, “The sun is going down and it will take us a while to get home. You were heading in the wrong direction. Are you okay walking in the dark?”

“Haha!” responded Lena. “We’re experts at walking in the dark! Do it all the time.”

Mitchie must have understood her sarcasm because it was getting a little too dark to see details, but they both heard the unmistakable “chi-chi-chi.”

“Follow me, then,” was Mitchie’s friendly command.

They trudged through more forest than they remembered coming through before and, as they walked, they questioned Mitchie about the mountain and whether there was an overhang.

“Better than that!” was his answer. “We were hoping you wanted to stay long enough for us to fix up a cave that’s over there. I think it will be just the right size!”

“Wow!” came the twins’ reaction. “A cave?

That's the best thing I could imagine." Franklin's enthusiasm even surprised himself.

"Only we don't want to compete with bears or mountain lions for it," was Lena's hesitant appraisal of the possibility.

"No worries," said Mitchie. "We'll talk about all that tomorrow."

Chapter 7

Circle in the Dark

They continued on with a fairly clear view of the ground and surroundings. The moon was fuller than it had been and was lighting the way nicely. It led them around several trees that Franklin traced with his eyes, wondering which of these thousands was the one they had tried to keep their eye on. Then they saw the dense forest open up into a clearing they thought was theirs, at first, but they quickly realized that this was definitely not the one they knew.

The moonbeams shown down in soft, translucent ribbons and illuminated a most incredible scene. They froze in astonishment, stopping at the tree line and barely hidden from view. There, in the middle of a great wilderness was a cozy, small open space surrounded by towering trees that seemed to be standing guard, like watchful soldiers around a community of bears who were still, focused, and sitting in a circle.

At first, Lena wondered if these were the "ghost grizzlies" she had heard of. Some people thought there were still a few grizzly bears in this wilderness, but no one had proof. But then she noticed their smaller size and darker color. These were black bears and much safer to be near. For some reason, neither sibling felt any fear, but just looked on in silent amazement as an unimaginable social event unfolded.

The moonbeams seemed to focus on a large bear at the far end of the circle. He looked old with scattered white hairs on his face and his position at the head of the round seating arrangement seemed significant. The rest of the bears were very young, they noticed. Little more than babies, but they were all transfixed by whatever the old bear was saying. They were in varying positions as they sat, but all were still. Some of the chubby little legs were crossed, some stuck straight out, a couple of cubs were on their sides propping their heads on fisted paws whose elbows were on the ground. They were just far enough away, and the senior bear was soft spoken enough that they couldn't make out what he was saying to them, but whatever it was must have been terribly interesting.

"Story time," explained Mitchie with a nod. "Want me to introduce you?" he offered in a whisper. "We need to wait until Koda is finished telling the story, though."

"Oh, wow! I don't know if I can handle all of this," whispered Franklin in wide-eyed reverence. He felt like an intruder; an intruder on something very special and something he wasn't sure he was supposed to even know. Lena didn't say a word, but just stared into the scene as the old bear adjusted his position and the little bears fell into more casual poses.

They heard Koda make an announcement that ended the session, and the audience of small learners began to pop up one by one. Koda stood up and motioned to a group. They could hear him say, "Cubby, Scoot, Luna, Spanky, come see me before you go."

The twins' feet were frozen on the mossy ground at the edge of the tree line while they watched four little cubs amble up to their leader and look at him intently while he talked softly to them. Franklin and Lena were very curious about what he was saying. Straining to hear, even leaning forward on their tiptoes, they still couldn't make out a word.

While the private conference was being held, Mitchie scurried right out into the middle of the clearing, making his presence obvious. A couple of the cubs looked at him and waved a paw. Two said hello to Mitchie. The twins then realized they were in the company of more friends.

Even though Mitchie had stepped boldly into their circle, they noticed that he waited patiently for Koda to finish talking with the four cubs. When the great bear was finished, he patted the youngsters' backs and sent them off, each heading in a slightly different direction. Franklin whispered to Lena that they must be headed back to different homes or dens for bed.

Once the last cub had left, Koda looked down at Mitchie and spoke. “Well, hello stranger. I haven't seen you in a few days.”

“I’ve been busy, and I think you’ll be very interested to know with what...or who,” answered Mitchie.

Koda cocked his head and gave Mitchie a quizzical look.

Mitchie looked over his shoulder back at where Franklin and Lena were still frozen in their tracks. “I would like to introduce you to... Come on out. I have someone very special to introduce you to.”

Mitchie’s gentlemanly command was easily followed. The twins slowly, but excitedly, stepped out into the clearing with full trust in Mitchie’s instincts and smiled their best smiles at the huge, grandfatherly bear who looked at them with unmistakable wisdom and kindness in his eyes.

With a tone of respect and formality, Mitchie gestured toward them and said, “Koda, I would like you to meet our generation’s humans--Franklin and Lena. They were lost in the woods when we found them. Franklin and Lena, meet Koda: the leader of our whole forest."

Lena found words sliding out of her astonished mouth for the first time in over half an hour. "Whoa. A king."

Koda took his seat again with a subtle, but deep chuckle. "We don't use titles around here, but it's interesting to see what you might compare me to," Koda responded with a wink.

Mitchie shifted the conversation by asking, "Koda, weren't you alive when the last human was here?"

"Yes, I was. I was young, but I have a few vivid memories. It was a young man who had just finished college and was out here hiking with a friend when he was badly hurt. We helped him heal and sent him on his way. The memories I have will never leave me, though." After a thoughtful pause, he added, "He was one of the trusted."

"The trusted," both twins thought simultaneously, followed by many questions that filled their minds, but they were hesitant to ask too much. Both felt like they were taking precious time from a very important being, so they weren't surprised when he stood back up on hind legs, causing him to tower over his visitors.

"Well, folks, it's very nice to meet you, but it's getting late. I think I'll be heading off to sleep. Let me know if I can help you." He turned and dropped to all fours just before he noticed it, but Franklin's late reaction had been to reach out awkwardly for a handshake. When the dark brown, shaggy mass came down in a graceful thud, Franklin dropped his hand and all he could think of to say was, "It was an honor to meet you, Sir!" The great bear nodded, turned slowly, and sauntered off into the black.

Lena turned to Mitchie. "He is amazing!"

"Yes, he is. Wait till you meet his mate, Ursula."

This created more anticipation in both siblings, but neither one said anything. They were both getting sleepy, so they headed back to the now-familiar leaf bed in their clearing. They would rest with even more amazing discoveries dancing around in their heads.

Chapter 8

Wishing For Fishing

As soon as they woke up, Franklin felt a sudden determination to find a more suitable place for them to sleep. Without admitting it out loud, they both were settling into their new habitat and were losing their ambition to find human civilization.

The chipmunks were scurrying around them and making sure they had breakfast. Franklin announced, "I am going to see if there's a good cave we can sleep in."

Mitchie, Pockie and Henna, Pockie's mother, suddenly popped up from around a corner. While Lena petted Pockie and visited with Henna, Franklin discussed the possibilities and potential obstacles in finding the right cave. Mitchie knew he had already mentioned a cave to him, but he recognized Franklin's ambition and chose not to say anything.

The animals noticed that, while Franklin was talking his plan through, he was sitting on a large rock, drawing in the dirt with a stick. This became his habit, which amused the animals and satisfied Franklin's urge to draw his experiences. By the time they were ready to leave, there, in the dirt, was an amazing likeness of Mitchie. Mitchie took a look at his portrait, gave a satisfied smile, and nodded.

Franklin asked Lena, "Are you okay staying with the chipmunks if Mitchie and I go search out a cave?"

"Sure!" Lena smiled at the two furry friends in her lap. "I'm good!"

After pocketing a few nuts and berries, Franklin and his dependable guide left the clearing, promising to be back before lunchtime. Meanwhile, Lena asked the new friends surrounding her if there was anything they could teach her. It just so happened that Henna, Nutalia, and Bellus had been hoping for this moment.

Lena told them how she and Franklin had wished to be able to catch some fish but needed hooks and some sort of line to do it. Henna was skilled at making tools from just about anything so, as soon as she heard this, she began to devise a plan for making fishhooks from the bones of animals that had died. She could give them to Lena, and they could catch some of the trout in their stream. As soon as the instructions began to unfold, Lena felt her mouth watering. Just the thought of fish, real meat, cooked and warm, sounded like heaven. She shook herself back to attention and listened carefully to every detail so she could participate in making this minor miracle come true.

Bellus, who had long, beautiful eyelashes and an extra sweet smile, led the way to the tree hollow where they had been storing supplies. The team of four began to bend, break, pull, stretch, fold, and weave. They enjoyed their girl time chat as they worked, and Lena was amazed to find all they had in common. They all loved their families, enjoyed the company of friends, and seemed to feel good when they helped each other. Lena had grown familiar with it but still giggled in her mind at times when she focused on their chopped, high-pitched speech. She thought they were the cutest sounds she had ever heard.

Where the work proved to be less efficient, she noticed that Nutalia would speak up, set directions for everyone, and push the project forward. Henna crept over close to Lena's side at one point and whispered, "Sometimes she gets called 'bossy,' but we know she means well, and she usually gets things done while everyone else is still just thinking about it."

This trust she shared was followed with a wink that assured Lena they were all the best of friends and respected each other. She must have wanted to explain her strong and spirited friend so Nutalia wouldn't be misunderstood.

Lena wasn't sure how they had accomplished it, but after a while, they had two strings of woven grasses with sharp hooks on the ends. With this sense of accomplishment, they took a work break, and Lena ran in circles with the younger chipmunks, laughing, playing, and learning each other's games of chase and tag. Henna spent her time putting away the tools and Bellus smoothed the fur on her head, arms, and sides with her tiny paws. At one point, Lena swore she saw Bellus rubbing berry juice on her tiny lips.

Not far, past the edge of the thicker woods, the land opened up to the hills and meadows where they had spotted the mountainside. Closing in on the area where the cave was carved into the mountain, Mitchie and Franklin had cautiously approached a family of mountain lions. Mitchie didn't know them and had introduced himself and the human while Franklin stood there shivering in his shoes.

The male, whose name was Banga, and who clearly was the leader of his pride, told them, in a slow, deep, and silky voice, that they were more than happy to share this cave because he had already found another place not far away. His growing family included three playful cubs who were tossing each other around like bean bags in the background while they talked. The cubs' mother was watching over them and stayed at a distance.

Franklin felt his body finally begin to relax, listening to the generous and curious cat who was eyeing him constantly and beginning to ask questions. Rather than feel intimidating, though, the questions seemed to come from genuine interest.

Franklin could see that Banga was not only strong, muscular, and tawny with muscles that rippled when he moved, but he was a smart feline that enjoyed learning new things. He asked questions about human technology because he had seen hikers at a distance with devices Franklin figured must have been radios and cell phones. The hikers had never known they had been watched. He asked about human family structure, customs, work and how they spend free time. After they had thanked him several times, the golden cats wandered off together and Franklin went immediately into the cave with Mitchie following close behind.

While Franklin decided it was a nice cave, Mitchie looked around at the familiar cave he had in mind all the while. He didn't realize a family of mountain lions had moved in, however, so their timing was perfect. The hole that would be their doorway was only about four feet in diameter, but it opened up into a fairly large room. His best calculation was that it was about seven feet high, five or six feet wide, and about fourteen feet deep. They could easily sleep in here and store their food. He couldn't wait to show Lena.

Lena was back at the clearing looking into the backpack he had left behind. She knew that they had put two sandwiches and a bottle of juice in it, but she wanted to remind herself what else Franklin had packed since it looked like they were going to be there for a while. Two jackets were rolled up and stuffed in, Franklin's pocketknife, a photo of them with their parents at their last birthday party, and a comb. A comb! She hadn't realized Franklin had packed his big, black hair comb because it hadn't looked like he had used it once! Lena had been running her fingers through her long, usually silky, dark hair from time to time to keep the tangles under control, but this was a big relief.

She sat and gently worked the teeth through every strand on her head until her hair was as sleek as she usually wore it. It gave her a great sense of satisfaction. It surprised her how clean her hair seemed after only being able to rinse it with water, and there was definitely no shampoo or soap in her brother's backpack.

When she finished combing, she noticed Bellus had been standing behind her watching her every move. The last item in the pack was a twenty-dollar bill that had been left tucked into one of Lena's birthday cards. She had been glad she had it with her when they first struck out on foot. Miss Carol told them she might take them to their favorite store and Lena had come prepared. Now, a paper bill seemed more useful for starting a fire than anything else. A fire. Now, that sounded pretty great. They could be warmer at night and actually cook some of their food for variety. Something warm in her belly sounded so nice after days of berries, nuts, and salads of strange greens and mushrooms.

Mitchie and Franklin made their way back just as Lena had decided to test her fishing skills. She, along with the help of Nutalia and Henna, had strung the hooks and were ready to head to the stream where the trout were. "Franklin!" she called when she saw her brother walk up. "Look what we made!" They exchanged stories about their morning experiences and then, a group headed to the stream.

Mitchie led them to the place where the trout were usually easy to find and they dropped in their hooks, hanging from long, broken branches that swung out over the water. Mitchie stood back with Henna and Nutalia, watching the anxious fishers who looked like they fully expected to catch something. After a while of silent observation, Mitchie asked, "What will make the fish want to bite your hooks?"

Franklin kept his gaze into the water, but answered, "Well, we're just hoping one will bite. If it does, we could use its guts for bait to catch more."

"Well, the second part of the plan sounds good," acknowledged Henna. "But I'm not too hopeful about the first part."

They continued to dangle the bone hooks into the water for about half an hour before their enthusiasm melted into discouragement. Lena finally suggested, "Are there any caterpillars or insects we could put on the hooks?"

"Now we're talking!" replied Nutalia. She and Henna scampered around until they found three beetles and a worm of some sort along the bank. Mitchie just watched, propped against a tree trunk.

They threaded the insects onto their hooks, lowered them into the water and watched hopefully. Time after time, however, the clever trout picked the bait off the hooks and swam off. The final piece of worm was lowered while they held their breath. Here came the trout. They saw him swim up to Lena's hook and the water was so clear she was able to watch carefully for the exact moment he opened his mouth and closed down. She was poised and ready, on a hair trigger with every muscle tightly wound. In the exact moment of the closing of the bite, she yanked extra hard. Her built-up tension poured into the fishing contraption all at once, pulling on the line faster and harder than she had meant to. The overreaction failed to hook the fish's mouth, but had, somehow, flipped the fish up into the air, landing it on the bank, only a foot from the water.

Before there was time to calculate an effective approach, both twins, instinctively, threw their entire bodies down on top of the trout, frantically trying to grasp him with their hands at the same time. The three chipmunks took a step back. Henna commented, "Well, they are certainly committed."

To their great sadness, the fish wiggled his way out of their combined grasp, flopped over to the water's edge and was gone before they could react again. They both let out bellows of frustration. To top it off, Lena saw that the hook that had taken hours of work to make was broken. "Ugh!! I want fish so bad!" cried Lena. Franklin knew better, because of the timing, but couldn't resist correcting her, "So badly." Lena rolled her eyes and threw the line & broken hook down onto the muddy bank of the stream.

Mitchie had been patiently watching the predictable scene play out. He knew how swift and clever trout could be. He also knew that Franklin and Lena were learning from this experience. Keeping his solution just out of their reach so they would continue to think, he tossed out, "It would be so nice if there was an easy way to catch these guys. I can see that you miss the taste of meat."

"I know," answered Lena in an exasperated voice, "but we don't have any fishing poles, real hooks, nets, nothing!"

Franklin was feeling angry and added, "If I had a baseball bat, we'd be eating some by now!"

Mitchie was quiet. Nutalia asked, "Does everyone want to head back or are we going to try another approach?"

Lena had been thinking and plopped down on the ground. The others joined her in response. After a long pause, she said, "A net of some kind would be better, but what could we use?"

Henna responded, "I guess we could weave more lines together and make a net out of them.

Lena's immediate reaction was, "Oh, that's crazy! That would take years! But then she added, "I'm sorry. That was rude. It really might work; it's just that it would take forever."

"Yeah," replied Henna. Nutalia chimed in, "It's all a matter of what you want most. We can make a net if everyone would be quiet and get to work."

Mitchie, who was still quietly observing, hinted, "If there was only something that could scoop...."

"Like what?" Franklin looked at the small critter next to him.

"Something that could move fast with sharp parts that could hang onto a slippery fish..." Mitchie added. The others were all sitting and scratching their heads at this point.

After moments of silence, Lena shouted. "Oh my gosh! Like a bear's paw!" She seemed pleased with herself while Franklin looked wide-eyed and hopeful. The group turned to Mitchie.

Mitchie's eyes grew large, and he smiled. "Now, that's an idea! And it just so happens that we have friends who have that very tool at the end of their arms! I know they would be more than happy to help us. Great thinking, Lena!"

It was late in the day by this time, but the twins couldn't wait to ask the bears for help. Maybe, by the next day, they could have fish for dinner. Mitchie led them to the bear community and said, "I will ask Koda who he will send to help us."

Franklin nodded asking, "I guess that's the chain of command?"

"Yes. I always go straight to him in these matters. He is in charge here and we must respect that. Besides, he'll know the fastest paws in the community. Chi chi chi." Mitchie gave them a wink.

The others stood back and let Mitchie cross the invisible line that marked the bears' territory. He promised to be back quickly, and he was. In just a few minutes, he returned, announcing, "Wrigley! He's sending Wrigley to help us fish tomorrow morning, and he may bring a friend!"

Lena felt her body reacting with true excitement. She jumped, clapped her hands, and cheered. Franklin kept repeating, "Thank you. Thank you."

That night, the twins slept more peacefully than they had since this whole adventure had begun. The stars were extra bright and seemed to smile down on them. They had found a cave but had decided to still sleep in the company of their new, trusted, and very helpful friends...at least for now.

CHAPTER 9

FIRE?

The next day started early with an enthusiastic leap out of the leaves. Franklin called for Mitchie to get the details on their fishing trip. Mitchie asked the twins, as they were eating their breakfast of berries, if they had thought about how they would eat the fish.

The quick paced chewing of excited children about to embark on another adventure suddenly slowed. The two looked at him and then at each other. With hesitancy and a wrinkled nose, Lena finally said, "I hear sushi is delicious."

Franklin chimed in, "I'm not eating raw fish. I have my pocketknife, and I remember enough of what Dad taught me about starting a fire that I think I'll be able to do it. We just haven't needed a fire yet since the weather's warm and we've been living off raw food."

Mitchie sat quietly thinking about this thing called fire for a while and then said, "You have to understand that animals feel very differently about fire than humans do. You use it because you can control it. We cannot. It is our instinct to run from it because it can ruin everything we have, even take our lives."

This was a very sobering thought the twins hadn't considered. Franklin's mind flashed back to images of forest fire warnings and his dad showing him Smokey Bear, a fire safety mascot from his generation. Lena thought of how they would eventually need fire if they stayed and how that might affect their relationship with the animals. Neither one wanted to do anything to put that at risk. These animals were their friends, and some were starting to feel like family.

Franklin explained, "I would definitely be very careful with the fire by making a dirt circle around it with no dry leaves close by to catch fire and I would put it out completely after we are through using it."

Lena asked, "How would we put it out?"

"By pouring water on it, of course," answered Franklin.

Lena countered, "And where is the bucket we would fill with water?"

Mitchie, again, was sitting back and watching the discussion go back and forth while he sat silently. After a moment of thought, Franklin offered, "We could throw piles of dirt on it. That would smother the fire."

Mitchie finally stepped in, "If you're fine with raw fish, we can go now. If you want to cook it, I will have to speak with Koda. It will probably require a community council meeting." He spoke the last words with a sober tone. It caused the twins to realize the seriousness of the favor they were about to ask.

Fire could be an incredibly useful thing. It could also destroy and terrify. The two siblings talked between themselves and decided that they would definitely honor the decision of the council. They had already developed a lot of respect for so many of the animals in the community. They had been directed, protected, trusted, taught, helped, and befriended by them. They would not disrespect their wishes on this issue, no matter how important it seemed to them.

Franklin spoke for them both. "We will wait to fish after the council has met if that is all right. We will honor their decision." Mitchie nodded and told them he would let Wrigley know what was going on. He might be near the water by now. Franklin and Lena thanked him for his help and Mitchie scampered off to take care of the matter at hand.

The rest of the day was spent with the usual gathering of the day's food supply, drinking from the stream, playing with their constant companion, Pockie, and learning the names and personalities of more of the chipmunk community. These interesting creatures were a very close-knit group and seemed to look out for each other. They heard Bellus, Nutalia, and other chipmunk mothers watching over the safety of other chipmunks' children and correct them when they got out of line. They all helped teach each other's children, too.

Nutalia, a natural leader who was an expert at gathering and cracking acorns and similar hard foods, gathered young chipmunks around her, coaching them until they were successful at cracking their own. Another mother, named Nuces, was teaching other youngsters how to dig and burrow efficiently.

Franklin was absolutely fascinated as he watched the little forest classes with students who were so eager to learn. He saw some that were not content unless they were helping a fellow chipmunk who found the task challenging. Other groups, he noticed, were competing to see who could do the tasks best or fastest. And others who took far longer than the rest because they wanted the job done perfectly. As they worked together and completed their assigned tasks, the word that came to his marveling mind was "harmony."

Mitchie told Franklin that the community council had set the meeting for the following evening after chores were done. The two of them sat on a fallen tree and watched the sunset together while Lena helped Henna and her friends fill a tree hollow with the nuts they had gathered.

The night was quieter than usual. As they finally walked to their beds, the twins barely spoke. The weight of the council's decision was on their minds. They were both starting to consider their futures more and knew that they would probably not survive a winter with their friends without fire to keep them warm.

Chapter 10

The Council Decision

The next day, the twins went swimming - well, as much as you can swim in a shallow stream. They stripped down to their underwear and ventured out onto the smooth, sun-warmed boulders, choosing the deepest spot they could find.

Watching the trout dart around them was frustrating and fascinating at the same time. Their delicious meal seemed to be toying with them. They were beautiful in their own way, slicing through the water with such grace as the sun glinted off their shiny scales.

When the twins found a spot between the smooth, weathered rocks that was about four feet deep, they slipped in. The water was quite cool, running off the high mountain top. Lena let out a small screech when the chill covered her body. Franklin acted tough, but the cold water made him bite his lip in surprise.

Lena whispered to Franklin at one point, "Look over there. We're being watched." It was little Cubby, Franklin's favorite young bear.

Cubby didn't say anything but just watched next to a tree near the shore as they splashed in the water. Cubby was easy to spot among the others in his group. He was the darkest black.

Franklin and Lena were surprised to discover how many shades of color there are among black bears. Some were as light as ginger, most were a darker brown, but they decided the species must have been named after the most beautiful ones; the blackest. Shy little Cubby usually showed up when Franklin was drawing his pictures in the dirt, but he was coming around more and more often, which made Franklin happy. Cubby watched every move Franklin made; especially when he had a tool for art in his hand.

After playing in the water for a while, they sat on the water's edge until their unders dried out, talking about what the council might decide. Lena had ideas of how they could persuade the animals that it would be safe, but Franklin pointed out that they really weren't one hundred percent sure it would be. Besides, he had never even started a fire by himself before.

Mitchie had explained earlier that when the council met, they were to wait in the chipmunk clearing. When it was almost over, Mitchie would come to escort them to the bear clearing where the meetings were held, to hear the decision. Representatives from each kind of animal in the area would be there and would be involved in the decision making. Franklin and Lena had thanked him and let him get back to his duties.

The rest of the day, Franklin went over and over in his mind the steps to start a fire. He visualized the materials he would need and walked through it all, along with all possible safety precautions his dad had taught him until he believed he would be prepared.

When the time came, the twins joined Pockie, Henna, and several of the other chipmunks for the wait. Some of the others that they were still getting to know came out to play games and keep them occupied. Rustle and Firby were leaders in charge of a game that reminded them of Simon Says, and Fergus, the community comic, told some chipmunk jokes. Fergus was a born clown. Even the way he moved was funny. They noticed that he was always surrounded by other giggling chipmunks and seemed to be a party on four legs.

The twins were tickled to hear a roar of "chi chi chis" go up from the gathered group, yet they did not understand one single joke. Their instinct was to laugh along, not wanting to appear rude, but their laughter turned out to be genuine because of how funny the whole situation struck them.

Lena was entertained, watching all of the different forms of laughter represented, while the parents were coaching the young ones on how to be good audience members, when to clap their paws and when to be quiet.

After Fergus' performance, he told the twins that laughter and humor are important to animals, too. He explained that different cultures find different things funny, that laughing relieves stress, helps them bond, and allows the joke-teller to share various ideas in a way that's easier for others to handle. And the joke-hearer can think about those ideas in a different way. They couldn't help but like this guy.

The party went on until the sun set, when Mitchie suddenly appeared in the midst of the fun. "All right, everyone, I will take Franklin and Lena to the council. Thank you for being good hosts. I hope Fergus told his lizard joke. Chi chi chi." Franklin made a mental note to find out about that later. "Everyone is free to go back to your homes now. We will announce the results to you in the morning."

The leaf litter crackled as everyone skittered off to their homes while Mitchie, Lena, and Franklin left for the revealing of the verdict. It surprised the twins as they trekked through the woods that were becoming familiar, how at ease they felt compared to when they had first arrived. They were recognizing open and bare spaces, a ravine, and dense tree clusters as they walked, making small talk as they went.

When they arrived at the bear clearing, the sight that unfolded between the tall timbers struck them with awe. This time, a doubled circle was filled with three or four representatives from the families of bears, chipmunks, mountain goats, mountain lions, elk, moose, bighorn sheep, mule deer, wild turkey, coyote, bobcat, lynx, marmots, pikas, grouse, doves, and other birds. Fireflies were twinkling in the background. They were stunned to see so many different types of animals in such a small space apparently cooperatively working together.

Most turned their heads, from their seated positions, toward the three of them as they approached. It was a little unnerving to have coyote and mountain lion eyes trained on them all at the same time. Koda was, again, at the head of the circle, but this time with an air of gravity that matched the focused faces of his audience. Lena reached out to hold onto her brother's arm. Mitchie stepped forward. "Everyone, this is Franklin and Lena. They are ready to hear your decision," he announced. Lena noticed a lump forming in her throat and Franklin's mouth went dry.

As if in slow motion, Koda stood up, looking very regal and imposing. He motioned to the twins. "Come over here, you two."

Franklin took the first step and Lena followed as they rounded the back of the circled group and up to the leader's side. Koda took his seat again and began to speak in a tone that calmed them. He spoke of the history of their rare relationships with humans, what a special occasion this was to be sharing their forest with the twins, the stories they had heard of other humans, and their instincts about fire. None in the council had any personal experience with fire and only one mountain lion knew a fellow cat who had been close to a fire years before. Their secondhand knowledge made fire a great mystery to them, yet a force to be respected.

Koda asked if they would describe this phenomenon to the group and explain their experiences with it. Franklin felt unsettled because he thought they had come to hear the decision and now it seemed like they had to convince the council themselves. He found himself looking at Lena, the Science Queen, as he had, teasingly called her more than once.

Lena sensed his expectations, cleared her throat, and began, "Fire is energy and matter. It's really an amazing thing and most people consider it mesmerizing and beautiful. It's just burning gases, basically, that create light which moves with the breeze while it flickers in red, orange, yellow, blue, and white. It can consume some solid things and melt others. It can't burn up water, though; it can only make it evaporate. It can be very useful when it is contained and controlled..." she paused briefly and then continued. "...but if it's not, it can kill and destroy." As the final words came out of her mouth, she realized she might be causing the loss of their opportunity, but she respected the animals too much to be anything less than perfectly honest.

The leadership had several questions, and one by one, began asking them, starting with Ramsey, the leader of the long-horn sheep and ending with Slake, the bobcat spokesperson.

When the questioning ended, they were a little surprised to see Ursula, Koda's mate, rise up and come forward. She presented herself in such a way that the only word Franklin or Lena could think of was "dignity." She stood by his side with poise and confidence as Koda addressed the group. Ursula looked at the twins as Koda explained that, while they had concerns, the council had agreed to allow them to try their fire experiment as long as proper safety measures were observed. The twins learned later that Mitchie had brought a strong argument in support of their wishes.

Franklin and Lena were relieved, honored, and excited, all at the same time. They thanked the group, promising they would be extremely careful, and Franklin found himself bowing, for some reason, as he thanked the elders. He laughed about it to Lena on the way back as he decided it must have been a subconscious gesture of honor but must have looked pretty silly. Mitchie overheard and told him the animals understood the respect he was showing, which eased Franklin's embarrassment a little.

The first thing Franklin did when they reached the chipmunk clearing was ask Lena if she was okay with sleeping in their cave that night. He had been storing his backpack there and wanted to get it. She knew exactly what this meant. He wanted to get to his pocketknife. She asked where he was planning to try starting his first fire and he smiled like a little boy who had been caught sneaking an extra cookie. Then he answered, "Just outside the cave in that bare spot where nothing's growing." She knew he'd be up with the sun in the morning to give it a try.

That night, as they entered the cave, Lena saw that her brother had been busy. He had taken berry juices along with soft, colored rock and had painted an entire scene on the cave wall. "When did you have time to do this?" she asked in amazement. She just couldn't believe it! The colors were limited, but he had managed to depict a grove of trees and four different animals all sitting together. In that moment, she thought it was the most beautiful artwork she had ever seen.

"This is your best yet, Brother," she said, standing back and appraising his work with a beaming smile.

Franklin looked down and mumbled, "Maybe that's how those hydro glyphs, or whatever they're called, got started."

"*Hydro* means *water*, you dork! Ancient cave drawings are *hieroglyphs*. Repeat after me…"

They laughed a while over that one, but that night they slept deeply and peacefully in their cleaned, swept, and cozy cave. It had been so cold at night that even burrowing deep into their leafy bed wasn't enough to keep them comfortable. This cave that insulated and blocked the wind made all the difference.

Even though Pockie had become their sleeping companion every night they stayed in the chipmunk clearing, Henna didn't allow him to venture to the cave overnight just yet. She knew how much Franklin and Lena loved his company, though, and in time, she decided she might allow a sleepover at the new place.

Sure enough, with the first light of day, Franklin sprang from the leaf bed, dug the pocketknife out of the backpack, picked up the flat pieces of flint he'd collected and stepped outside the cave. He took a few steps before he remembered how he had promised to be extremely safe. Being that safe meant having his sister there in case anything unexpected happened and he needed help. He stepped back toward the cave and saw, through the shadowed interior, his sleepy sister yawning and stretching. "You need me, don't you?" Lena said in a sassy but loving way.

Franklin nodded. "We really do need to do everything we can to be super safe. They trust us."

As soon as he heard himself say it, Franklin and Lena both recognized the familiar words. Was this part of what Koda had meant when he spoke of the special humans? Could they be some of "the trusted?" Or maybe they were *becoming* some of the trusted...*IF* they did this right. Franklin settled his excitement a bit as they sat down and talked through the steps they would follow and how they would handle any problems.

Just at the moment they decided to have Mitchie join them, a loud clap of thunder startled the twins, coming out of the blue and splitting the quiet air. They hadn't paid attention to the cloudy sky, but before they could react, rain was coming down on them like a gym class shower. A few seconds later they were safely standing back inside the cave opening and feeling thankful they hadn't been far from it.

"Thank goodness we found this cave!" Lena exclaimed as she shook off the few drops that had landed on her.

"You mean thank goodness your *brother* found the cave!" Franklin threw these words at her with an edge of sarcasm. She rolled her eyes but acknowledged that it had been his idea first.

The rain came hard and steady for about an hour. The twins sat down and watched their first rain in the wilderness as it washed the landscape, cooled the air, and filled it with a sweet smell. It refreshed everything around them. This changed their plans for the day, but they didn't mind. Their talk turned to reliving some of their last days' adventures. They finally made sense of the cartoon-like sounds they had heard that first day. Everything since had been surreal. They agreed that they would never have had a dream quite like their new reality.

The next day, with renewed determination, they struck out early to try the long-awaited challenge of making fire. Franklin had had an idea during the night and was scanning the mountainside for a sheep. He explained to Lena who had been calling Mitchie, that if a sheep would allow him to cut off a little wool with his knife, it could make starting the fire much easier. She helped him search until they found two longhorn sheep together, climbing a ledge above them. The siblings approached them tentatively as two strangers about to ask a favor, but they quickly discovered the surefooted creatures were happy to see them. Spook and Flibbity said that Ramsey, their leader, had already told their group all about them. The sheep introduced themselves, listened to the young man's plea, and generously answered, "You can have as much wool as you want."

It took Franklin a while to pull and gently cut each pinch of wool, determined not to hurt the friendly donors. He was glad he had sharpened his knife on the rocks so the blade would cut easily. Spook and Flibbity stood as still as castle guards while the boy took slice after slice of their thick, soft, cream-colored wool and handed them to Lena who kept asking, "Are you sure you don't mind?"

Flibbity was the most talkative and assured them that they were excited to be helping. Lena had turned up the bottom of her shirt, creating a big pouch. Once it was full, they thanked the sheep several times, who had turned to resume their climb, and then the twins made their way to the bare spot where they planned to use it.

Just outside the cave, where the brush was cleared away and the dirt made a safe floor, they found Mitchie awaiting their return. Lena proudly showed him the wool in her shirttail while Franklin explained his idea. Franklin took out his pocketknife along with the flint rocks he had found and started to work. Lena scooped up dirt into a pile by Franklin's so that, when they finished, they would have a sure way to put out the fire. Since she knew fire needed oxygen to burn, she realized that Franklin had been right; they didn't really need water, just a way to smother the fire. Franklin had gathered dead limbs and twigs because Lena reminded him that dead wood was the driest and easiest to catch fire. At one point she overheard him mumbling something about wishing he had joined the Scouts.

Lena built the ring of dirt around the fire space, just as her brother had described. She watched as her brother tried striking the rocks on his knife blade, the reverse, then flint on flint. He got some sparks eventually, but it took several patient tries before he got the wool he was using for tinder to catch fire. After that, it was a matter of quickly adding dry pine needles one by one to get an actual flame.

Franklin learned, through trial and error, to blow steadily, but not too hard, on the lit wool and then, basically, add wood, from the smallest pieces to the largest. After the needles, he added a small piece of a twig and, when the fire seemed stable, he added a big handful of dry leaves and needles. He built his way up to larger branches to build the fire's size, strength, and endurance. He told Lena it felt like bringing something to life and then having to keep it breathing.

"Yes!" Franklin shouted in victory.

Pockie, who had stayed at the cave but had recently appeared and was now transfixed with the project, clapped his paws together and made little clicking noises that clearly expressed delight.

Lena's reaction was to quickly gather extra nearby twigs as if the need to keep the thing alive was desperate. Mitchie stepped back at first, watched quietly and then rejoined them, staring breathlessly at the glowing flames that danced on its stage of branches. What a magnificent thing they had accomplished. This could change so much for them. Now, they could cook their food and keep themselves warm on colder nights.

Mitchie announced, "This calls for a celebration!" As the words came out of his mouth, he realized that he was contradicting an instinct about this new wild thing, but he was mesmerized by it, just as Lena had said, and happy for his friends.

Mitchie knew the twins would want to stay by their fire for a while, keeping it going to extend their success, so he asked if he could bring other animals to see. They agreed on how to showcase the magic and Mitchie left to gather a crowd.

Lena immediately began to brainstorm ideas for cooking while Franklin listened and stoked his fire. He couldn't help but think of how proud his dad would be. The thoughts made him a little melancholy, but also proud of himself. "I'm proud of us, Lena." She nodded, knowing what he meant.

The two sat quietly together, staring into the flickering light, and thought separate but similar thoughts, side by side.

It wasn't long before they heard them coming. Trampling through the forest came creatures on four legs, all under Mitchie's clear direction. The twins overheard his warnings about a safe distance and where to stand so they could all see. He had them all in a line that, at one point, turned into a circle. Soon, they were all wrapped around the outside of the blazing wonder. Franklin and Lena felt very proud and admired the fire themselves, but they could see, in the eyes of their new community members, even more amazement.

At Mitchie's direction, the crowd cheered in unison, filling the air with energy that felt electric. Several animals stepped up to make comments directly to the twins. Ramsey was particularly impressed and expressed pride in his team's contribution of wool. Flibbity was with him and promised to give a detailed report to Spook, who had opted to stay home.

After most of the animal audience left, their next feat was trying to cook fish! They noticed that only one bear had come, and they hadn't recognized him. Franklin asked Mitchie if he thought Wrigley was still available with his fishing talents and, as soon as the question was asked, Mitchie was off like a shot to get him. It seemed like only minutes had gone by when Wrigley and one of his bear buddies came pounding up to them with six fresh trout.

The siblings were glad they hadn't put the fire out yet. One looked at the large mess of fish and Lena couldn't help but laugh. "Who were you guys fishing for?" she asked.

Wrigley and his buddy, Slash, looked at each other and shrugged their shoulders. Lena told them she supposed big bears ate that much, but these fish were large enough that one apiece was plenty for the two of them. Franklin spoke up, thanking the bears profusely and invited their helpers to join them and eat the other four trout.

Wrigley and Slash sat down while the twins took turns scraping off fish scales with the pocketknife and while Lena devised skewers from sticks to roast the fish over the flames. When they had turned to reach for the other four fish, they noticed those were nowhere to be seen but saw their friends wearing expressions that seemed to ask a clueless question, "What?" as they licked their lips. They hadn't waited for theirs to be cooked.

After the siblings gave each other a side-eyed wink, they dove into their dinner. It was pure heaven when they took those first bites. Both moaned as their teeth sank into the fresh, white, warm fish flesh. Lena closed her eyes and shook her head back and forth as she chewed. Franklin answered with, "Mmm, best fish ever!" After four or five bites, they were lost in a mood of sheer bliss, got the giggles, and started laughing at themselves.

After a moment, they suddenly became conscious of their audience and felt a little embarrassed in front of the creatures who eat fish every day like it's no big deal. The perplexed way Slash was staring at them made them laugh so hard, they fell backward, and it took a while before they could catch their breath and finish picking every last morsel of meat off the delicate fish bones.

They discovered that if they picked carefully, they could eat around the bones and avoid the organs in the middle. They were glad Lena's plan worked because, even if they were good at fileting fish, they didn't have a pan to cook them in. Whole fish on sticks was the solution they were both satisfied with and would use the method time after time.

Chapter 11

A Dangerous Experiment

As the days passed, the twins became quite familiar with a forest that had once seemed like an impossible evergreen maze. They made a daily trek from their cave, where they now slept every night, to the chipmunk clearing to begin their day's activities. Franklin was spending a lot of time with his little buddy, Cubby, and though they didn't talk much, Franklin knew the little bear was watching his every move - especially when he painted or dirt-sketched. Henna had begun allowing Pockic to spend the nights with them and they were happy to have his snuggly company again.

When they first started making trips to the cave, there had always been a chipmunk available to escort them and make sure they didn't get lost, but now they knew that path well and had become friendly with Buck and his herd who had come across several times. The little elk calves were growing larger and less shy. Franklin especially liked them. They would dart off when Lena approached them, but for some reason, they allowed Franklin to pet their heads and backs without straying away. Lena reminded him about his way with animals."

Before they had become more sure-footed, the twins loved watching the calves' cute antics, especially when little Calvin would try to scratch his neck with a hind leg hoof and topple over after losing his balance. He seemed perplexed at how easy it was for his mother to do it. The female cows made sure the twins knew how important the elk were to the community. One thing they were responsible for was foraging on a lot of the underbrush which not only made natural and random forest fires less likely but also made room for fresh plants and more animals.

The twins had become friends with more chipmunks and were learning their individual personalities. The chipmunk pups were still drinking their mother's milk and it was the cutest thing to watch. They drank and drank and then passed out for a while like they were in a happy coma. They were growing bigger and beginning to develop more fat on their bodies which would give them better insulation when the cold weather came. It also made them look terribly cute.

Lena added to her scientific knowledge that most animals in the wild gave birth in the spring when more resources were available. That explained why there were so many parents of all kinds with babies all at once. What surprised Lena most was how quickly they were all growing. It caused her to think they must grow and become independent faster than people because of their shorter life span. Pockie's developing independence was a good example.

Franklin was right; Lena was frequently wishing for a camera to capture all the very special things that were happening to them and all the beauty in the wilderness. She decided that no mansion was as beautiful as their current home.

It dawned on the twins one day that they had completely missed the last two weeks of school and were well into summer. The surprising thing was that no people had shown up to rescue them. Now, they were hoping no one would.

They had noticed a couple of small planes flying overhead, but they didn't seem to be searching - at least as far as they could tell. The twins had always watched out for planes when they built their fires. To keep their smoke from being spotted, they agreed to put the fires out immediately if they saw a plane coming and to build most of their fires at night when it was dark, and most planes wouldn't be flying over.

Franklin had shown real foresight in packing jackets while the weather was so warm, but there had been cool nights when they were very glad to have them. Depending on how long they stayed, those extra layers could eventually be life savers.

Lena had relaxed enough to start practicing her singing and the chipmunks and birds gathered around her when she did. Her parents had encouraged this talent that she hadn't used in a while. It felt good to exercise it again. Franklin teased her about being like Snow White singing in the forest, but it reminded her of the school plays where she had an audience. These days, the audience was a little different, but Pockie was always in the front row.

Franklin became quite proficient at building fires and had proven himself to be very safe, to the satisfaction of most of the animals. The ones who weren't thrilled with the idea just kept their distance when it was time to cook. They had a fishing routine established with the bears who happily took turns scooping fish out of the stream for them. In return, the twins watched over their cubs and played games with them while their parents rested or played by themselves.

Franklin had another idea one night for how to use his fire to fashion bowls of wood they could transport water in, and for holding other things. He remembered learning that some Native Americans had made dugout canoes by burning out the insides of logs. Once the vision of creating a bowl came to him, he became determined to make it a reality. He searched until he found some large chunks of wood from a fallen tree and slowly rolled them around in a bed of coals until the outsides were charred and easy to scrape off with his knife. It was a long process that took lots of time and patience, but he was noticing that his focus and resilience were becoming stronger since they had been in this wild habitat. He felt proud of himself.

Once the outside was in a reasonable shape, he set out to burn a hollow in the middle. When he began this next step, the wood caught fire all right, but the flames grew more quickly than he anticipated, leapt out, and scorched his chin, causing a reaction that sent the flaming bowl-to-be flying over the dirt circle and into some dry brush. All at once, the ground caught fire and Franklin panicked.

Lena was right there and, after they let out a few screams and a word they didn't normally say, they both took a deep breath and began to systematically scoop and drop, scoop and drop their handy pile of dirt onto the burning dry grasses, leaves, and needles. It seemed like the flames were outmaneuvering them no matter how fast they worked, and they both scrambled in fear, trying to leash this monster that had broken free and was running away. The growing flames were just about to reach a tree when they both dumped dirt at the same moment that, luckily, put out the last of the threat.

Panting from panicked breathlessness, Lena exclaimed, "I'm so glad none of the animals were here to see that!"

"That was a close call," Franklin acknowledged breathing heavily and dusting the dirt off his hands.

They stood there silently for a while with their hearts banging in their chests thinking about what *could* have happened.

When Franklin finally looked up, to his horror, standing about ten feet away, just watching, was Koda. He had never felt so guilty. Lena noticed his expression and had followed his eyes to see their observer. The twins stood there sheepishly with dirty hands and stunned faces, while trills of smoke were rising from the charred leaves around them. This was it. They had blown their chance for, not only fire, but probably to be counted among "the trusted."

Koda was quiet for a long time and the twins stood there, frozen. The great bear finally walked over to the cleared area and sat down. He motioned for the twins to join him. Franklin was searching and searching his mind for the right words, but everything sounded stupid to him, so he remained silent.

"What is your plan now?" Koda tilted his head.

That triggered Franklin to start anxiously tripping over his words with apologies and offering to never start a fire again.

Koda responded, "So, that's it? You don't plan to try again?"

After a doubt-loaded pause, Franklin's question came back, "Would you *let* us?"

"Only if you've learned a lesson that you wouldn't repeat," came the answer.

Then Franklin's nerves caused his volume and speed to pick up. "Oh, yes sir! I learned a lesson for sure! I wouldn't let the flames get so big! I would blow them out constantly and restart it so it wouldn't get that out of hand. Just a tiny little fire inside!" Lena pressed her lips together and determined not to say anything just yet.

After a silent, deep breath, Koda told them he had watched the whole thing and saw that the fire had been started because of a lack of knowledge, but not carelessness. He could see that Franklin was keeping his word about safety. He gave credit to Lena, too, for having the piles of dirt on hand. The twins felt their shoulders lower a bit and Franklin felt the moisture in his eyes drying.

When the conversation was done, Koda offered to stay while Franklin tried again. The first bowl was a loss, but after the learning experience and giving it more thought, he wound up with two large bowls that would serve them well. The repurposed chunks of a tree stump were saving them a lot of trips to the stream and were highly valued by the two of them but would never be as valued as Koda.

Chapter 12

What Was That?

Lena, who had really had a hard time adjusting to feeling dirty constantly, had figured out a schedule for alternately washing their outer clothes and underwear in the stream in the evenings and letting them dry overnight while they slept. They did this about every three days, and she just lived with the grit the on the other days. Franklin didn't seem bothered at all by the dirt. Lena settled the official timing of the wash with, "Whenever I smell you, it's wash day."

She asked Franklin why, since he bothered to bring his comb, he had not packed their toothbrushes. His explanation turned out to be a good one. If those had been missing from the bathroom when they left, Miss Carol would have known that they had run away and would have called the police sooner.

The way he planned it, she might not notice the twins missing for a while and then would probably assume they were at a friend's or something and not be alarmed. This would give them more of a head start.

Lena cleverly devised toothbrushes for them by fraying the ends of twigs like Franklin had done to make paint brushes. There was no toothpaste, of course, but water and a good scrubbing were better than nothing, she decided.

They agreed that the most important thing that had been happening, though, was spending time with Ursula. She had proven to be wise, kind, patient, and the perfect leadership partner for Koda. They were a respectable pair together and the twins could see why all the animal community looked to them when big decisions needed to be made.

For a few days, they had daily visits with her where she gave them a chance to talk about what was happening in their lives. Lena showed her the picture of them with their parents. They talked and she listened. That was how the visits went until day three.

Franklin decided to tell her that there were nights when Lena cried herself to sleep thinking of their parents. Then, Ursula began to ask them questions. Franklin asked her if something was wrong with him since he wasn't crying like she was. He knew he loved his parents as much as Lena did. Ursula explained things to him like the fact that there are different personalities that get expressed differently and the influence his culture might have on him.

She still mostly listened though. The twins always felt better after these visits.

They were accomplishing, learning, and even healing, but something was missing. They had received so much help from the animals that they wanted to help them now that they felt more secure in their survival skills. These were things they talked about at night as they were falling asleep. One night they decided they would ask Koda the next day if there was something they could do to help the community.

As soon as the morning sun shone through the cave door, the twins sprang up, tended to their morning routines, and set out to find Koda. Pockie woke up after the twins had eaten breakfast and were leaving, but he noticed they saved him a few berries. He gobbled them down and took off behind the twins, chippering, "Wait for me! Wait for me!" They chatted excitedly about what jobs Koda might assign them, but truly had no idea what they would be.

Pockie, who had caught up and reminded them that his locating instincts were better than theirs, led the way to Koda. He was deep in thought and sitting on a log when they arrived.

"Hi, Koda!" called Franklin.

"Well, good morning to you," responded the bear who shifted his massive weight as he looked up.

"We want to ask you about something," Franklin added.

"Well, come on over here and have a seat," Koda coaxed.

The three sat in a semi-circle at his feet and began explaining their thoughts about helping out. They asked him if the last human who had been there had helped them as a way of thanking them. Koda reminded them that the hiker had been hurt, and he didn't remember him being able to help. Koda recalled that his name was Ben, and his parents had liked him very much. All his parents had talked about was getting Ben back on his feet so he could go home. As he spoke of the hiker, the twins could see that his mind was wandering back to things he hadn't thought of for a long time. It made Koda smile. "Ben had a huge red backpack - so big, it could eat your little backpack for a snack!" he chuckled. He also recalled how the hiker had a foldable fishing pole in it, a little butane lighter, and many other things that made his stay much easier than theirs.

Lena redirected the conversation back to what they had come for. She repeated Franklin's question about helping. Koda scratched his head, was quiet a moment, but then said, “You may not want to think about the day you leave yet, but there are some important things you can help people understand better...”

They were interrupted when, suddenly, behind them, a loud crack of snapping twigs caught their attention. Franklin and Lena were startled by how quickly Koda stood up on his hind legs and spun around toward the noise. They all froze for a suspended moment. After listening for clues, Koda called out into the silence, “Who’s there?”

The twins thought at the same time, “I thought he knew everything.”

No response came back. “Something’s not right,” said Koda with a grave expression.

"Do you think it might be someone looking for us?" Franklin finally whispered.

"No. It's not a human," Koda answered. He let his weight fall and, as his forepaws hit the ground, something moved away from behind the near trees. They could all tell. What it was, they didn't know, but Koda said it was not any animal he knew. And he knew every animal in their forest.

That night, an emergency council meeting was held. The twins could only wonder what was discussed, but realized they felt surprisingly safe in the company of their forest friends. While they ate and prepared for bed, they talked about how strange it was to see Koda's concern. He had always been so calm and had the confidence of someone who had everything completely under control. Whatever this noise had been clearly worried him. He said it wasn't human, though. That was their biggest fear, but apparently, not his.

They fell asleep that night with questions, but trust that let them sleep soundly.

Chapter 13

Hide!

Lena usually sprang up first each morning and started gathering food while Franklin enjoyed starting his days more slowly. Sometimes he liked to sit just inside the thickest edge of the woods, where it felt more private, to just relax and look around. He noticed, in his spot, that the sunlight randomly poked through the undergrowth and hit the forest floor, but not often. The majority of it was shaded and hidden. He smelled the slightly musty odor of the dew-moistened ground litter but was beginning to pick up subtle scents of different animals, too. He realized, one day, that they hadn't seen any signs of human life, other than the planes, since that first night when they had stepped over a few smashed drink bottles and cans. Everything here was pristine, so peaceful and so beautiful.

While Franklin sat in his hideaway, an occasional bird or squirrel would visit, but no words were spoken. It was his refuge and nature could sense it. He loved hearing the distant chirping of the birds while he observed chunks of pine on the ground with little holes bored into them. From time to time, small beetles would poke their heads up from the holes and then hide again.

The trees grew oddly, too. Franklin noticed how many trees don't grow straight up. Every time he had drawn a tree, it was standing straight and tall, but these trees in the dense woods were too crowded for that. With all of the undergrowth, they had to search for sunlight and were growing at odd angles under the canopy. Some were growing almost parallel to the ground at the bottoms of the trunks and then, where they could find sunlight, turned, and grew upward. This fascinated him. He would never draw trees the same.

He listened to the rhythmic whoosh and alternating rattle that the breeze caused. He noticed that the young, tender leaves were higher and held onto their branches with tight vigor, while the floor was covered with brown ones that had served their turns, had loosened, fallen, and were slowly decaying to nourish the soil while being buried to make room for the layers to come.

One day, just as the morning routines were underway, Lena heard an unusual noise. It had become so unfamiliar that it took her a second to realize it was the sound of men talking. She stopped in her tracks and looked around to see where Franklin was. Since she couldn't see him, she guessed he must be in his underbrush hideaway. Her immediate reaction was to hide. This was the moment she could be rescued, yet her instinct was to hide. She listened carefully and tried to assess where these men were.

Their voices were coming from the left side of their mountain, and they seemed to be about fifty yards away. Even though her brother was a quiet person in general, she knew that the last thing they could afford was for him to suddenly call out to her, Mitchie or anyone else, so she crept over to his spot and gave him their silence signal. They had rehearsed this signal many times when they were younger and played hide & seek with their parents, so he knew immediately what it meant. She snuck between the vines and fallen limbs to join him and, as they sat there, their shared look made them realize more than they had before; they didn't *want* to be rescued.

Once they recognized that they both felt that way, a fear began to rise in them. They must not be found! They separately thought this must be the cause of the noise they had heard the evening before. Why couldn't Koda tell it was men? It dawned on them that, while they had thought about planes seeing their fires, they hadn't considered someone just walking up. Evidence of their fires was right out there in plain view. Not only that, but there might even be tracks from their shoes. If these men went into the cave, they would see the leaf beds, backpack, and things they had collected or made. They sat there for almost an hour with a feeling like rocks were in their chests. They squeezed each other's arms for comfort.

Suddenly, Mitchie appeared on a tree trunk just above them. "They're gone," he announced.

"You saw them?" Lena asked anxiously.

"Yes. They were hikers who had veered off their trail somehow. I followed them for a while until it looked like they got their bearings again. I guess that's the closest anyone has come in years...besides you," he said with a wink and a chi-chi-chi.

When Lena told Mitchie of her guess at their distance, he assured her that they were actually about twice as far away. "Sound travels farther out here than you're probably used to," he said.

Franklin noted, "That experience makes me very nervous. "We'll have to start cleaning up traces of our fires each time and making sure we don't leave any footprints or other clues out in the open."

Mitchie told them the men hadn't been on their side of the mountain's edge and had missed their camp completely, but he agreed they needed to be more careful in the future. This close call surprised Mitchie, who would have to make sure Koda knew.

When he was told, Koda called another council meeting. Lena and Franklin sat in the cave, nervously going through all of the possibilities of what they might discuss. Would they decide having humans in their space was too risky? Would they ask them to leave? If they did, how would the twins find their way out? So many things swirled around in their minds. It felt like a swarm of bees were narrowing in and about to start stinging.

Lena suddenly held up her hand as if to stop the venomous mob and shouted, "We're gonna be okay! This will all work out. We've made it this far. Who would have ever thought we'd be living weeks in the middle of nowhere with a bunch of animals? True, some are pretty cute, but some are predators, don't forget."

Franklin jumped up at that point, grabbed onto his sister with an extra rough hug and added, "We can do this together! You're right. Just keep our heads on."

Then, they found themselves pacing back and forth in the cave. It was nighttime when all council meetings were held, and the temperature was dropping. They rubbed their arms to keep warm as they paced. After a couple of hours and no one had come to give them any news, they fell into their beds and went to sleep.

The next day, they went about their usual routines and noticed that nobody said a word about the meeting. They both decided not to bring it up, hoping that they had worried for nothing. All this made Franklin even more determined to find a way to help the community. He thought about it day and night now.

While he was picking and sorting some dandelion leaves, Cubby appeared about ten feet away from him. He had learned that the adorable cub would probably not say anything if he didn't start the conversation. The bear might stumble around a while and then disappear. But with a little coaxing, Franklin was pretty good at getting him to talk. He noticed that when Cubby was with other animals he was usually quiet, too. But when he did speak, everyone around him stopped and listened. The one thing that made it easier for him to talk was when Franklin was doodling in the dirt with a stick. Cubby would usually get very close, watch for a while, and then ask questions about the pictures that always surprised Franklin.

That day, once Franklin got him to open up, Cubby asked him about the stars in the sky and if he saw pictures in them. This opened up a whole conversation about constellations and connect-the-dot pictures that seemed to fascinate Cubby.

The next day, he found Cubby drawing dots in the dirt with a stick and then, joining them with lines. Moments like these made Franklin feel like Cubby was much more than a little bear. They seemed to share things in common that Franklin couldn't express.

While Franklin's attachments to the animals and their new wilderness life were growing deeper, Lena was beginning to think about their life back in human civilization. She thought about it most nights as they were falling asleep now.

When she would ask Franklin questions like, "I wonder what the Amish people will say when we get there?" he would usually ignore her. One time she asked if he thought there was any chance they would send them away or call the police and she noticed that Franklin became very agitated. He answered, "Well, we'd have to be able to be helpful if we expect to be able to stick around and be fed." The gruffness in his response was unmistakable. Lena wondered where that came from, but she didn't ask.

Chapter 14

Not Alone

Franklin woke up one day with noticeable determination and fresh energy, announcing, "I'm going to see Koda today. If I'm not back by the time the sun's straight overhead, ask Pockie or Mitchie to bring you over."

He usually spent the morning with her, making sure they had enough to eat, and she was fine before he ventured out, but this morning, he left without breakfast. He trekked through the woods until he came to the bear clearing. The first bear he saw was Slash and he asked him if he would mind getting Koda.

Wrigley was their go-to friend for fishing, but Slash was a great backup helper who fished with particular vigor. They loved watching him swipe his paws through the water on the days they went with the fishers to the stream. Even though his catch was often a little more mangled than Wrigley's, the twins found so much entertainment in his style. They decided torn up fish was worth it.

Slash was loud, rough, and larger than most of the other bears, but had a heart of gold and they decided he would probably help anyone who needed it. They called him a teddy bear behind his back and winked when they did.

Slash was glad to run this errand for him, and, in no time, Koda was ambling around the corner and headed straight Franklin's way. For just a second, Franklin had a flashing thought of how he would have responded to seeing a large bear walking toward him in a forest months ago. It was an amazing thing to consider how comfortable he felt in that moment, how much he had learned, how much he had changed.

As Koda reached Franklin in an open field spotted with trees, movement in the distance caught their attention. When they turned their heads simultaneously to see what it was, Franklin found himself stunned while Koda slowly, and with almost no movement, settled the doubt, "*That's* what we heard a couple of days ago."

The vision, not of a man, but of a strange, very large bear, lighter in color and with a more pointed snout than Franklin had grown familiar with, brought a sobering realization to Koda. This was a ghost grizzly, and they were not friends. Koda told Franklin not to move a muscle. They sat watching to see what the grizzly would do. Franklin had so many questions, but he knew not to talk. He couldn't help but wonder where Lena was though. The thought of her being out there, unaware of the intruder, made his heart race. In his mind, he kept saying, "Stay where you are, Lena. Stay where you are."

The bear began to walk straight toward them. It was obvious he had seen them. What was he going to do? What was Koda going to do? Franklin broke into a cold sweat now, but he remained still and stood next to Koda who was on all fours but, even so, almost as tall as him.

When the grizzly got within ten yards of them and Franklin was about to lose it, Koda swiftly stood up and roared. It was the most earth quaking; air shaking roar Franklin could have fathomed. It came up from the bottom of the great bear and shook the trees as it sounded alarm and intimidation throughout the field and into the forest. The grizzly stopped, looked at him for a moment and then slowly turned and walked away.

Franklin was paralyzed until the bear was out of sight and then fell onto Koda like a broken doll.

"He'll be back," Koda said in a solemn voice.

"Where did he come from?! I thought they were extinct! Why didn't he talk?!" So many questions were banging around in Franklin's mind and spilling out of his mouth.

Koda just said, "Let's go back." The two walked side-by-side back to the clearing where Franklin was relieved to find Lena. He ran up to her and began to breathlessly relay the details of their encounter. "Koda said it was a ghost grizzly! I remember you mentioning them, but we thought they were extinct!"

As Franklin went on & on, Lena listened with part of her brain and, with the other, was reflecting on what she had read about these bears. She recalled that the last grizzly anywhere around there was supposed to have been shot in the 1950s, but somewhere around 1977 or so, a hunter was mauled by one. The man survived to tell that it was definitely a grizzly and ever since, there have been sightings of grizzlies by individuals on rare occasions. Their existence has not been confirmed by scientists, so it's a bit like the Loch Ness Monster or Bigfoot legends. She wasn't sure if Franklin would know the difference between a grizzly and an unknown black bear, but Koda certainly would. This was serious.

While the twins talked, Koda alerted the others and called for another council meeting. The twins knew that these meetings were held on a regular basis, as needed, but they were definitely being needed more and more lately. Franklin hoped it was not caused by their presence. He wondered about the natural effect they were having on the forest, and he felt a strange kind of responsibility for the troubles.

The twins stuck close to Koda the rest of the day, and, for the first time, he invited them to the council meeting that night. It was such an honor to be included in this leadership meeting, but it was also a sign of the gravity of the situation in the forest they had begun to call home.

The animal leaders formed their circles in the moonlight and sat in their official places, while the twins positioned themselves next to Koda. After the introductions and acknowledging Franklin and Lena's presence, Ramsey, head of the longhorn sheep, began the questions and asked for protection for the more vulnerable species like his own. Koda spelled out the plan, including the hierarchy for who would cover whom.

The animals nodded in agreement. They contemplated the possible number of grizzlies or whether it was one lone bear.

The council planned every detail, and because of that, the twins felt safer as they learned what their expected role would be and how they would be defended. When they were allowed to ask a question, Franklin turned to Koda, "Why didn't he talk or why didn't you talk with him?"

Koda explained that, while all animals have the ability to talk, some outside their community choose not to. It's a sign they don't want to cooperate, and he could tell immediately that this bear would not be talking.

The two went back to their cave that night with heavy thoughts. Slash had been assigned to them and would sleep at the cave entrance for protection. Lena told her brother that she wasn't that scared but was sad to find out that not all animals were innocent and kind like the ones in their forest. Slash overheard what she was saying but stayed quiet and hung his head. She had imagined the whole world of animals being ideal until that day and she choked a little on the truth she had learned.

The next day, at Lena's insistence, they went to see Ursula. Lena had awakened pacing the cave until Franklin asked her why she was so hyper. All she said was, "We need to talk to Ursula. We just need to talk to Ursula."

When they arrived, the bear was waiting almost as if she expected the visit. Lena was the first to speak as they sat down. They had talked to her a lot about their parents, and she had helped them so much with her warmth and understanding, but today Lena's mind was racing with thoughts about their safety. She had gone to sleep feeling calm but had nightmares that awakened her in a panic.

She had horrible thoughts about her brother being killed - in her mind, the only person she had left - by this savage bear or maybe even a sleuth of bears. In her frenzy, she explained, "I can't stand to just sit around and wait for something bad to happen! I can't lose my brother! I think what I should do is have our bears watch over me from behind some trees and let me walk around out there till the grizzly comes after me and then the bears can kill him. I could be like the bait!" Franklin and Ursula could see that Lena had worked herself up into feeling completely frantic.

Franklin reached out to squeeze her arm saying, "I'm okay, Sis."

Ursula began, "We are all born with two important gifts to develop and use. One is logic; for learning, solving problems, and making sense of things. It's our black and white, facts-dependent side that is often related to math and science. The other is emotion; for feeling the powerful things that make life rich, for loving and appreciating beautiful things, and for expressing ourselves. It's full of color and it's often related to music and art.

"We need both gifts. They balance each other and should work together as partners. One of life's challenges is finding that balance, though. If we only use emotion, life can get out of control very quickly and we can put ourselves in danger. But, if we only use logic, we miss the things that make life worth living. We have to think *and* feel - together. Does this make sense?"

"I think so," they both agreed simultaneously, after a pause. They turned to each other and winked. "Twin moment."

Ursula looked at Lena and asked, "Where does your logic come from?"

Lena squinted her eyes, turned her head sideways, but hesitated.

"Touch the place where it comes from...on your body," Ursula prompted.

Lena slowly raised her hand and touched her head, looking at the motherly bear with a question mark in her eyes.

"Exactly," Ursula replied in a soft, soothing voice. "And that is your..." she coaxed.

"My brain?" Lena answered.

"Yes. Your brain. Now," she continued, turning to look at Franklin. "Where do your emotions come from?"

Franklin looked around a bit and then, hesitantly, placed a hand on his chest.

Ursula responded, "And that is your..."

Franklin took over, "My heart," he answered with questioning in his voice.

Ursula looked at *him*, questioningly now. "Your heart?"

By now, Lena was intrigued but remained quiet. Her eyes were darting back and forth between Ursula and her brother, anxious to see the outcome of this interaction.

After several seconds of silence, Lena couldn't stand it anymore and jumped in, "Your heart is just an organ that pumps blood to the rest of your body."

Franklin looked at her and nodded. "Yeah, it doesn't have feelings. I guess emotions come from our brains, too," Franklin added.

Ursula explained, "They're both from the same place and equally important. And if you don't understand your emotions, it can affect your logic. For example, if someone were feeling upset or panicked about something, those emotions could drive them to do something that might interfere with them using logic or thinking that would normally keep them safe. Does that make sense?"

There was a long silence. Neither twin said anything. Ursula remained as calm as always and just sat with them as they considered her question. Finally, she asked, "Do you think this idea came from a balance of your emotion and logic, Lena?" Again, there was a silence.

Lena let out a deep breath and admitted, "I guess not."

Franklin felt relieved that Lena was calming down, but, at the same time, felt something rising in him that he had been struggling with in the back of his mind for weeks. It boiled out of him, unexpectedly, in words that were louder than he'd intended. "I have to be the dad now! I *have* to work hard to take care of us. Plus, you have helped us so much, Ursula. I *have* to be a man and help you back somehow and protect you now!"

A stunned look took over Lena's face. "Well, *that* was out of the blue!"

Immediately, Ursula gave her a look that put her on pause. "Whoa. That's a big burden," Ursula acknowledged solemnly. It was very unlike Lena to be quiet, but the cocked head and raised eyebrows Ursula had given her, left her completely silent.

After a while with no one speaking, Ursula started to hum softly a soothing tune. They had no idea bears could make music so hearing this rare lullaby made them both feel a kind of happiness that relaxed them. The two felt their bodies slowly falling into the warm, furry comfort of Ursula's chest. She held onto them for a long, long time. It was quiet, calming, and magical as Franklin considered the craziness of his finding consolation in a large, wild bear.

When they finally stirred to stand up and leave Ursula's presence, they were amazed at how much better they felt. Neither one felt the need to say anything about what the other had mentioned during their visit. They just went back to business as usual, preparing their next meal and playing with the smaller animals, but watching over their shoulders for any intruders.

Chapter 15

Watching and Waiting

The next day, Slash appeared from around the corner as the twins woke up. "Where have you been?" questioned Lena, slightly worried about their safety.

"I was right here but checking out some smells and a sound from over there." He pointed to his right.

"What did you hear?"

Slash told them he thought the grizzly had been there during the night and had come as close as about five yards from the cave. This caused a shiver to crawl up their spines and the three of them decided to find Koda. Lena quietly wondered why Slash didn't notice until he woke up. She thought he would, somehow, know immediately if the intruder had gotten close. The thought was unsettling.

When they found Koda, he was in his den with Ursula. Slash told them what he had discovered. Koda revealed that other animals had also come to him with evidence of the grizzly's return. They had decided it was most likely only one bear because all of the paw prints and droppings were the same.

Koda's advice was to make things look like business as usual, but to be on constant watch and remember the plans they had set in place. He decided that another council meeting might make them too vulnerable, not knowing who might be listening in now. Just to be safe, he sent his messengers, one-by-one, to deliver communication to the different groups.

Franklin and Lena were on pins and needles all day, but there was no sign of the strange bear, and they went to bed that night feeling safe, tucked behind their door guardian, Slash, who filled the space entirely. If anything or anyone wanted to get to them, they would have to step on him first.

The following day, the weather was extra nice. Franklin wasn't good at predicting temperatures, but he knew it was cooler than the days before and it put him in the mood to draw. With Slash in the distance and Lena organizing the cave's food storage, he gathered his knife and special drawing sticks and set up a space for creating near a rock he could sit comfortably on.

No sooner did he outline the perimeter of what would be his scene, than Cubby came waddling up to watch. Franklin loved this little guy. He smiled every time he came into sight. Cubby would be the inspiration for today's drawing.

"Good morning, little buddy!" Franklin greeted.

"Hi," Cubby responded shyly. The two sat quietly as Franklin began to first sketch trees out of the dirt. He handed Cubby a stick and silently guided him to sketch a tree into the scene himself. Cubby seemed unsteady at first, but later, pleased with his results.

Then, Franklin began to outline what would be a portrait of Cubby sitting in a patch of flowers. It didn't take Cubby long to guess what the focus of the drawing was, and he looked up at Franklin with a smile. "Let's see if I can do this!" Franklin said. Cubby gave a satisfied nod.

Franklin sketched and sketched until a detailed, but monochrome scene unfolded. Then he said, "If these are going to be flowers, we need a little color, don't we?" Cubby smiled. Franklin stood up and looked around. "I'm thinking that if we can scrape some minerals of different colors off these rocks with my knife, that just might do the trick!" He wandered to a piece of limestone and picked up a dark rock he didn't recognize but knew it would contrast with the reddish iron ore dirt he was sketching into. Cubby was full of anticipation as he watched Franklin in the distance scouting out nature's art supplies.

Their carefree smiles suddenly froze as a noise crackled from the patch of trees between them and the hair stood up on the back of Franklin's neck. Cubby bristled, too, and they locked eyes with each other over the many yards' distance between them. Before either of them could react, the ghost grizzly walked right out in front of them. Franklin could see he was larger than the black bears now. He just stood there, boldly, with his massive, muscular body projecting the very image of power.

How could he have gotten so close without them noticing? Should he yell for Slash? Was Lena still in the cave? Panic rose in Franklin and his thoughts were so jumbled, he wasn't sure what to do. He was facing the bear but looked through the side of his eyes to the cave and thought he saw part of Slash's fur at the entrance. Maybe he was there. Hopefully, he was there with Lena, but he wasn't sure. It was just far enough away that he wasn't positive.

Frozen in his tracks, Franklin's eyes began to dart back and forth from the cave, to Cubby, to this enemy while his mind raced with options for what to do next. Then, he counted as the grizzly took three steps toward them, and it didn't seem to be stopping.

While Franklin was still processing what was happening, Cubby suddenly took off like a bullet. Franklin was stunned. He had no idea Cubby could move so fast. The cub ran right out into the open path between them and this beast and then veered to the right and continued past the grizzly! What was he thinking?

"Cubby!" Franklin screamed. Then, he found his own legs were flying, running faster than he had ever run before, toward his little buddy. His mind knew what would happen next but he couldn't seem to stop himself. He was barely aware of a roar in the background but kept barreling toward Cubby. A few seconds later, he could see, in his peripheral vision, the grizzly coming toward them. And he wasn't walking.

Adrenaline and instinct had taken over and Franklin was almost within reaching distance of Cubby who was flying even faster, if that was possible. The grizzly was getting closer and closer. Now, he could hear the heavy, rhythmic breathing of the enemy and the thud of his paws hitting and shaking the ground beside him.

They were running almost parallel. The bear was so close that Franklin could smell it. He pushed himself as hard as he could, with all of his mental and physical strength, to gain speed, but the grizzly was only getting closer, almost touching him.

Then Lena's terrified scream came shattering the air from a distance as Franklin was finally close enough to reach Cubby. But he felt something hit his left leg with tremendous force and he lost his balance, falling and loosening his grip on Cubby who jumped up a nearby tree.

Before he could grasp what was happening, he looked up to see a tangle of bears, he wasn't sure how many. They were slashing, roaring, and sending blows only about five or six feet away from him.

His first instinct was to roll sideways away from the fray. It wasn't until the fight was over and a lifeless bear lay in the field that he looked down at his leg. His jeans were ripped from the top of his thigh to his knee, and, beneath the fabric, his leg had a rip to match. The odd thing was, it didn't really hurt.

He saw blood everywhere but just sat there stunned until his sister and all the animals ran over and gathered around him. His first words were, "Is Cubby all right?"

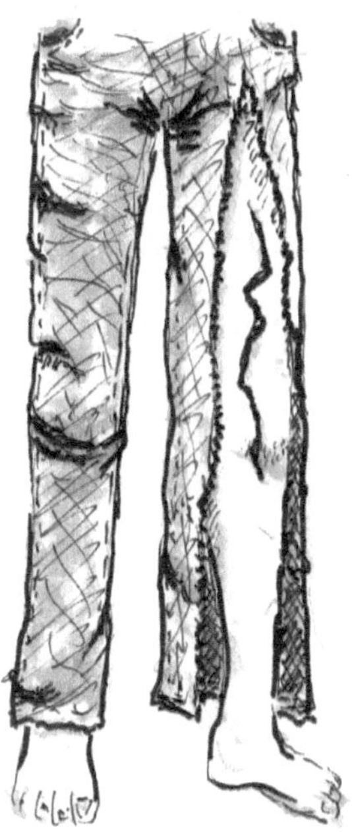

Lena let Ursula bring Cubby over to assure Franklin he was fine and to explain that Slash and the other bears had saved them. Slash was the first one on the scene. The one he saw lying dead was the grizzly.

Lena's thoughts made her head pound. Her brother's leg looked bad. Bad enough that she had to consider getting him to a hospital, which would be the end of their freedom. Blood was everywhere. She knew he might need surgery and would need antibiotics because it was almost certain this would get infected. But how could she get him there? Where *was* the hospital? The ghost grizzlies were most likely truly extinct now, but they had problems on their hands they were not prepared for.

By now, the pain hit Franklin. He grit his teeth. "Okie dokie. I think it hurts now," he teased in a high-pitched voice with very wide eyes. Ursula told him that he had been in shock and so had his leg. It was waking up now and might not be fun to live with for a while.

Henna and Nutalia immediately began scurrying around and Ursula told the twins that these "girls" knew what to do. Nutalia told Lena to heat as much water as she could on a fire. The competent sounding command made Lena jump up from her brother's side, but it hit her that she had not started a fire by herself before. She looked down at Franklin and he said, "Don't worry. I'll walk you through it. You can do it."

She was about to run and get the supplies from the cave when Mitchie said, "You don't need to build a fire over here. We need to figure out a way to get him to the cave and you can build it in the usual spot." This made sense to Lena, but it took them a minute to come up with a plan.

Franklin looked over to the cave which seemed, to him, to be about thirty to forty yards away. He calculated distances these days based on football field yardage and thought he was pretty accurate. He knew he couldn't crawl that far, now that the pain was starting to bolt through his body like burning metal. He began to shake all over and felt cold. Ursula was right there, holding his head and told him, "This is normal. It's shock." She warmed him with her furry arms and talked in soothing tones while they waited on a plan.

Pockie was actually the first with the idea of sliding a pallet of long, parallel sticks under him and dragging him to the cave. It was awkward, but they decided it would work. Lena bragged and bragged on him, and Henna was proud of her son's contribution. Franklin wanted so badly to be brave, thank everyone, and make jokes, but he found he couldn't talk for a while. All of his focus went to managing the pain.

It wasn't long before Bellus and Nutalia showed up with paws full of something. They told Franklin to eat it, which he immediately did, trusting anything with desperation. It tasted like moss and leaves, but, in a few minutes, a calm came over him that seemed miraculous. Then, the pain began to weaken. He asked what in the world they gave him and the two just stood there smiling and said, in unison, “special herbs.”

As a group, they decided that Lena had the hands to best grab the sticks and, once they got Franklin on the pallet, she was able to slide it, fairly easily, through the low spots on the ground, dragging her brother over to their cave. He instructed her, step by step, on how to get a spark, light the wool, and get a fire started. She realized that she had learned more than she knew and took over, at a certain point, making a beautiful, roaring fire.

Neither Franklin nor Lena had wanted to look too closely at the wound. They both knew that grizzly claws were two to four inches long and the power that was behind them could easily kill in one blow. They knew Franklin must have been on the outside of the bear’s swipe range, which was why he was alive, but they were both afraid to see bone or extreme muscle damage, which would mean he might not be the same again if he lived through this.

While the water was heating, Lena asked her brother, “Do you think we should try to find a hospital?”

"Are you crazy?" was his immediate response. "No telling how many miles we are from a hospital and there's no way I can travel that far. Whatever is done, must be done here." Then he pushed back a little further into Ursula's arms and said with a slight air of spunk, "I'm down for it."

Lena shook her head, but realized he was probably making the most sense, so she went to work. She got the water almost boiling in the bowls, let it cool, and Henna and Nutalia gave instructions on how to wash out the wound. Lena decided to leave her brother with the dignity of his pants but ripped them from the tear at his knee to the bottom so she could fold the fabric completely out of the way for the cleaning. "Well, there goes my winter leg protection," Franklin sighed. Lena reminded him that the giant rip had already spoiled that.

About that time, Bellus showed up with some brown-looking clumps in her paws. She told them that Mitchie let everyone know what they needed, and they had all gathered roots and stem parts from a grape plant she insisted they use. Several chipmunks lined up to offer their full paws to Lena.

When she washed out the blood and particles of dirt, her face lit up. "Franklin! It's not nearly as deep as I thought it might be!"

Relief washed over his face and the faces of everyone surrounding them. This made a huge difference in his recovery. They just had to focus on keeping it from becoming infected and Lena was determined to keep that from happening.

She spread the chipmunks' concoction over the wound, which was about fourteen inches long and looked like a long red lightning bolt. Thankfully, the herbs, whatever they were, were keeping the pain under control and Franklin only winced as she spread the salve over the wound. Bellus told them the grape stem salve would fight against infection, which brought Lena great encouragement. She was kneeling and working from her brother's left side and, after a while of focusing on his leg, Franklin looked to his right. There, sitting still and mournful, was little Cubby.

"Aww, Cubby. How are you doing? I was so scared for you. If anything would have happened to you..." Franklin was talking away, but noticed Cubby wasn't looking up. "Cubby?" He still looked down. It occurred to Franklin that maybe Cubby felt responsible for him getting hurt. "I'm gonna be fine, you know? This happens to people all the time and they get well. I'll be walking in no time!"

Cubby finally looked up. "I'm sorry."

"Sorry for what?" Franklin asked.

"I should have stayed still, but I thought I could get the grizzly away from you."

Oh gosh! This little guy wasn't running out of fear. He was trying to save me. "Come here, little buddy" he coaxed the cub. Franklin reached out and pulled Cubby up onto his chest and hugged him for a long time. "You're my hero," Franklin finally said. Cubby burrowed his face into Franklin's chest. "I'm gonna need you around to help me heal. Can you do that for me?" Franklin asked.

"You bet!" Cubby answered. Then the cub climbed off Franklin's chest and wandered off. "Wow" thought Franklin. He just shook his head.

As soon as Cubby left, Pockie took over the snuggling. Franklin was surrounded with love and knew he would be all right. Lena was the one who did the worrying.

Days went by and the chipmunk moms continued to bring him special herbs whenever Lena had to clean and re-dress his wound. She knew it should have been sewn up, but there were no tools for that. The open gash left more opportunity for dirt to get in, which is the enemy of a healing wound. As it began to scab over, Franklin decided he would like having a battle wound. The scar this would leave was going to be a serious one and a real conversation piece. It made him feel tough when he looked at it now. A grizzly scar. Whoa.

Chapter 16

Fighting Another Enemy

One day, Franklin sent Pockie to get Ursula. He felt the need to talk with her, but couldn't get to her den yet. Around noon, she showed up at their cave entrance. Lena met her and invited her in.

"It's an honor to have you here, Ursula."

"I'm happy to come and see your home." After glancing around their surroundings, she offered approval, "This is very nice." She admired Franklin's mural for a while and then sat, asking what was on his mind.

Franklin took a minute to think of how to begin his questions. "Koda said some animals choose not to talk and that means they don't want to cooperate."

"That's true," she responded. "You must be thinking about the grizzly."

"Yes," he confirmed. Franklin went on, "I wish he had said something. Anything. Because maybe we could have worked something out."

"Exactly," Ursula agreed. She began, "True communication is one of the most valuable things there is, but it's not easy. It requires understanding, humility, and the ability to really listen. Not everyone is capable of that. It's the only way you can really know another being or for them to know you though. The real you. We are very lucky here in our forest to all share the value of trying to understand another's point of view. It's a constant challenge.

"We have to teach it to our young. We all start off wanting everyone else to understand *our* view. It's natural when you're a child. As we grow, though, we should be able to look outside ourselves more and more. To be willing to talk would have meant the bear was willing to hear also."

Franklin thought for a while.

Ursula let him sit for a minute and then added, "We teach our young that the ability to express your thoughts and opinions freely is one of our highest goals. But if we want to have the freedom to share who we are, that must be respected. We show respect to the ideas of others, and they show respect to ours. If I constantly talk, I am just repeating things I already know, but if I listen and consider what another says, then I may learn something new."

They were quiet another while together.

She continued, "It looks like your parents taught you many of the things we teach our children."

He looked up at her. "Can you tell?"

"Yes."

This brought Franklin comfort and gave him more to think about.

"Your parents are not here, but they gave you many gifts that have already seen you through a lot and will see you through all you will face in the future."

Lena, who was listening close by, smiled at this assurance. After a while, the matronly bear left their company, but they always felt her presence in the woods.

Two days later, when Lena woke up, she found Franklin tossing and moaning in his leaf bed, but he didn't seem conscious yet. She went to check on him and he didn't seem right. She looked down at his leg and saw oozing yellow pus. Certain infection. She felt Franklin's forehead and he definitely had a fever. This was it. Exactly what she had been afraid of. She ran to the forest and called on all of their friends for help. She needed more herbs for the salve that had antiseptic and antibiotic qualities which had worked so well before.

The chipmunks went into fast action as Lena headed back to the cave. She gave her brother cool water to drink and prepared a fire to heat more water for the wound. Her skills had sharpened, and she was swift and accurate. While Franklin was becoming aware of what was going on, the water was ready, and she went into action. She prepared him for cleaning the wound and poured the warm water in. After washing her hands, she began scrubbing pus from the open wound.

"Yow!! I thought you wanted to help me!" yelled Franklin.

"I know it hurts, but we've got to scrub out this infection before it gets worse," insisted Lena. "I just wish we had some medicine...." she mumbled under her breath.

"You're not kidding!" Franklin yelped, just in time to see Henna, Bellus and Nutalia walk in with their herbs and the mud-colored ointment.

Though he was trying to be tough, Lena could see her brother was worried. She reminded him that pus is a good thing. His leg was like a battlefield after a battle where his white blood cells had been the soldiers fighting the infection and now lay dead after their victory. There were more battles to win before this war was over, but she didn't mention that part.

Franklin reached toward the three helpers, gulped down the herbs and gritted his teeth until they started to work their magic, but Lena didn't pause a moment.

"I'm sorry this hurts, brother, but I'm fighting *my* bear now." She was merciless, scrubbing and scrubbing while he lay there on his back as helpless as a turtle flipped over on its shell. Even though she was only focused on her mission, Lena felt Franklin beginning to shake. She looked up at his face and saw it distorted with pain. After a few more scrubs, he was trembling so much it felt like his body would vibrate out of her hands, but he didn't say a word, just bit his lip and stayed silent.

Lena felt an intense sadness for her brother, but she noticed that her determination to help him was stronger than the temptation to stop. She continued her job while Franklin shook in agony.

It felt like thousands of knife blades were stabbing his leg and his teeth were chattering uncontrollably.

After a while, the intensity of the cleaning slowed, and Lena began to pause and appraise the leg between scrubs. Only after the washing was complete did he finally begin to sense the help of the herbs.

While the trembling settled down, Franklin realized that he had developed serious trust in his sister, or he would never have let her do this to him.

Finally, the main work was done, and Lena took the mud salve and began to gently spread it into the jagged lightning bolt while Franklin wiped away the pain tears that had leaked out of his eyes and down his neck.

After the twins had calmed, they thanked the friends that surrounded them. How would they have survived without them? They wouldn't have, they decided.

Franklin's breathing slowed and he agreed to drink the water that Lena kept pushing on him. They were both finding strength within themselves that they didn't know they had.

Lena was surprised at how much she was willing to do for her brother. At home, she had refused many times to help him with his chores and usually didn't have any desire to do the little things he asked her for. The thought of how things used to be made her laugh a little. Franklin asked her what was funny, but she just said, "Oh, nothing."

Lena continued to bring him food and water and hardly slept at night, checking his fever constantly. She knew she couldn't tell his exact temperature, but she could tell his forehead got hotter at night and that made it hard for her to sleep. Pockie was right there, too. He was helpless, but knew how to stand watch, which he did with true dedication. He was a faithful buddy who got his pay for being guardian on the occasions when Franklin still felt like rubbing his head.

On the third day, Franklin's fever finally broke. Lena had dozed off a while before the sun came up and when she woke up, he was covered with sweat but was cool and feeling much better. "Cool as a cucumber," their grandmother would have said. "Thank God!" Lena called out into the echoing cave. This was a breakthrough, and it encouraged her to issue her brother a challenge.

"Franklin, today's the day you are going to start walking," she boldly announced.

"It is?" he questioned doubtfully.

"It is!"

After breakfast, Lena pulled him up by the arms and helped him get his balance on his strong right leg. She looked down for a moment at his other one. It pained her that she had had to scrub off the scab that had formed so nicely, in order to scrub out the infection, but it had healed over again, and a new scab had formed.

"Okay, lean on me," she commanded. Together, they figured out an awkward rhythm to get him to move. When it came time to put weight on the sore leg, Franklin felt like yelling, but he didn't. He just made a tense groan that let Lena know this wasn't easy. "Can you do this?" she asked, now more patiently.

"Yes. Let's go further," he nodded.

So, the two of them did a clumsy dance through the cave and out to some sunshine, which Franklin was so happy to see.

This was how the next several days began, going a little further each time until Franklin's strength returned and he was able to manage walking on his own. The day that happened was a day of real celebration. As much as he appreciated all that Lena had done for him, he had not been able to get any time alone in a long time and he really missed it. He looked forward to climbing back into his hideout. The hard part was bending his knee, and it took a while before he could kneel and take over the fire building again. Lena was happy to let him take that work back when the time came, though.

Weeks went by and Franklin's leg healed beautifully. He was quite proud of the jagged lightning bolt he had earned through his bravery but was annoyed with the flapping jeans legs that they had not figured out how to sew up. He wanted to just rip the long flap off, but decided with fall coming, he would regret it later. So, he walked around with one normal-looking leg and one that he decided looked like a superhero. It had a bolt of lightning on the front and was trailed behind by a flapping cape.

He spent more and more time with Cubby, teaching him to draw and Cubby loved every minute. Pockie seemed to be growing up the fastest. He was as sweet as ever but was spending more time with his friends. They both learned, after the attack, that Slash had come immediately to Franklin's rescue and had taken the brunt of the grizzly's wrath. He was wounded badly but had healed while Franklin was healing.

They had all been solemn about having to kill like that for the first time and were anxious to get the ghost grizzly's carcass out of their forest afterward. No one mentioned it after that. Life seemed normal again and the twins were beginning to plan for the fall. Time was flying by and they knew the warm weather would end abruptly. They knew that if they planned to survive, they would have to be prepared.

Chapter 17

What's That Sound?

They were leaving a visit session with Ursula one afternoon when they heard the sudden sounds of many creatures heading towards them at once. They went from calm to alert in an instant. Mitchie ran to the group that had formed. "A human! A human is getting close! Everyone, hide!"

The crowds of animals were coming from the direction of Lena and Franklin's cave, so they knew their usual refuge was not an option. With no place to hide, they frantically searched in circles for some place to keep them from this person's view in case they came closer. Ursula was right behind them. Mitchie, right at their feet, pointed out a low hanging branch in a nearby tree, but none of the animals were talking.

It suddenly dawned on the twins that all of their friends had gone into their protective mode of silence or using only the animal noises humans expected to hear. Franklin waited a second for Mitchie to explain, but then realized that his pointing was all the help they would get for a while.

Franklin motioned to Lena and boosted her until she could pull herself up onto the tree branch. Then he found Ursula underneath him, lifting him just high enough that he was able to pull himself up, too. They stretched and climbed from limb to limb until they were about twelve feet from the ground, according to Lena's estimation. The animals had disappeared as if there was another dimension they could retreat to.

The twins felt so vulnerable and exposed. It seemed like they could be seen as easily as they could see the forest around them when, over a hill came a red backpack. They held their breath instinctively while a man, looking equipped to hike for days, came steadily in their direction. He was looking from side to side and calling, "Boris, Bernadette, anybody here?... Boris?"

They sat frozen and in utter amazement. Did he lose his hiking partners? That wouldn't be a good thing. Did this mean he would stay in the area a while until he found them, or would he keep moving on? So many questions went through their minds. They finally let out a slow breath before they passed out, but the hiker was right underneath them.

It dawned on Franklin, at this point, that people usually look straight ahead of them when they're walking and not up into trees, so he began to relax a tiny bit. Lena was just out of his reach, but he looked at her to see if she was all right and to make sure she wasn't about to sneeze or anything. The first animal they were aware of was a bird they didn't know, but, from a branch just above him, Franklin could tell it was winking reassurance to him. The twins glanced back and forth from each other to the hiker until he was several yards away. The hiker was still calling names into the wild.

What happened next shocked the two of them so much, they couldn't move or speak if they'd wanted to. Koda appeared out of nowhere, walking up behind the hiker. Many things raced through their minds, but none of them made the twins feel comfortable. What was he doing? They didn't want Koda to hurt the backpacker just to keep them safe. They didn't even want him to scare the man, really. What was Koda up to? He was gaining on the man, and they couldn't believe it when he was only about eight feet from the guy and hadn't been noticed.

Suddenly, Koda snapped a twig and it seemed to be on purpose. The hiker turned around and saw the giant, old bear within reach and he froze. The man began stumbling over his words, but talked nervously to Koda, saying, "I'm Ben. I was here twenty years ago and...."

"I know," Koda interrupted. "Boris and Bernadette were my parents."

"Oh, wow!" The hiker who took a step back and stood in stunned silence.

Koda continued, "I was sensing that you were one of the trusted and then I recognized that gigantic, red backpack. Ben. It's good to see you again. I'm Koda."

The hiker's face brightened. "Little Koda?" he asked, now smiling, and dropping his gear. "I guess we've both changed a bit."

Sitting, still in silence, the twins listened and watched as this unbelievable situation unfolded before them. The reuniting of animal with the last generation of trusted human. Their muscles and breathing relaxed, but their minds were spinning with how this would affect their new life. Lena was focused on the thrill of seeing another person, while Franklin was experiencing an unexplainable pang of jealousy, wondering if this visitor would take away the friendships they had developed.

They listened as this Ben fellow explained that every year since he had been there, he took a week off work and came out here trying to find his animal friends again, but never had. He supposed the trauma of his injury had affected his navigation and sense of direction at the time, making it hard to retrace the same steps later.

The twins could tell he was truly excited to find the bear who was a little cub when he was last in their community. It began to warm their hearts and they decided that maybe he wasn't an enemy after all.

Ben was listing all the names he remembered, telling what he recalled from his time there and asking about several animals that were no longer living. He paused in solemn silence for a while and then continued his updates, including the fact that his leg had healed completely, and he had resumed hiking shortly after his time there.

Hiker Ben paused in the middle of recounting events that, clearly, meant a lot to him, shifted the atmosphere, and asked, "Has the community had any more humans in your world since then?"

Koda answered, "As a matter of fact..." he turned and looked up into the tree not far from them, commanding, "Come on down, it's safe."

By this point, both of them were anxious to meet this guy. The sense of threat had subsided, and they were intrigued. He looked about forty years old, had an impressive beard, and was dressed for the occasion, unlike them.

Lena leaned over to Franklin and whispered, "Pick a name!" as they began to scramble down the tree, jumping the last step and trotting up to shake hands. Ben looked completely stunned. This was the last thing he expected to see in a place he had tried to relocate to for twenty years. Lena was first to step up in her stained shirt and torn, purple pants.

"Hi! I'm Hannah," she said, with boldness and the confidence that caused Franklin to suddenly realize what she had whispered to him. He reached out his hand, reminding himself of the firm handshake his dad had taught him, since he hadn't had a chance to practice it in a while. "I'm Jake."

They looked to Koda to make sure he wouldn't give them away. Their thoughts were suddenly in harmony, realizing that their names might be in the news and people might be searching for them. The last thing they wanted now was to be rescued by the police and forced to live with strangers. Ben seemed to believe the contrived names and shook their hands with vigor and a huge smile. He had bright, white teeth and kind, dark brown eyes - as dark as Lena's.

An immediate, breathless conversation began as they asked Ben about his time there years before. He explained how the animals had cared for him, protected and fed him while his leg healed. It had been broken and deeply cut when he had tripped and fallen into a steep ravine.

Franklin told him he had fallen in one too and thought he'd had a concussion. This was the first time Lena heard him speak of that night and didn't realize he had thought the same things she had.

Ben looked down at Franklin's leg and said, "Looks like you have quite a leg story yourself! What happened here?" Franklin decided the true story wouldn't give away their identity, so he launched into the full tale, sparing no details. Ben was amazed and asked many questions about the ghost grizzly he had wondered about himself. Koda had sensed their reasoning and didn't give their identities away, for which they were grateful. This gave them time to think of what their plan would be. They were winging it now and dodged Ben's question of how they came to be out there until he approached it again.

When she could tell the questioning was not going to go away, Lena went into story mode and began a tall tale of abusive parents they escaped from and were trying to figure out where to go next when they got lost. Ben listened intently and didn't ask any more about it. Their conversation then included Koda who was sitting on his haunches at this point.

Out of the blue, he slapped his leg, laughed, and said, "That beat up old backpack is still with you?"

"Yep." Ben smiled with pride. "It was with me when I was here before and that experience changed my life. I keep it as a reminder." Reaching out to pat the pack, he added with a chuckle, "Plus, I paid a lot of money for this baby back in the day!"

About that time, Mitchie, Pockie, and many of their other friends came and gathered around as the twins introduced them to their next human. "This is a new generation, Ben, and they're great!" Franklin exclaimed.

Koda had put everyone at ease about the hiker and they all reacted with enthusiasm, ready to welcome their next guest.

Slash was in the crowd and spoke up, "There aren't any more hikers with you, are there?"

"No," Ben assured him. "I am all alone. In fact, my wife and kids don't know exactly where I am. They don't know why I come out here alone every year; they just know it's important to me. I can't get a signal out here with my phone though, so it's just me."

Koda spoke, "You mean you haven't told your family about us?"

"That was the deal, Koda. I promised to never tell a single human to keep your confidence and I haven't. It's been a weird kind of burden, but honestly believe it's best. They can't understand it like I do since they haven't had the experience and it would preoccupy them in ways that wouldn't be good for them."

This was sobering for the twins to hear. They had thought many times about how they wouldn't be able to tell anyone either, but they hadn't considered that it might even include their spouses and children one day. This made them, suddenly, extra glad to have Hiker Ben join them, a fellow human they could share this with.

After visiting a while, Ben took a look at the twins, leaned back a bit, and asked, "How long has it been since you guys have had some chocolate?"

"What?!" the twins yelled in unison.

Ben unzipped a compartment in his huge backpack and pulled out two power bars with a chocolate base, nuts, oats, the works!

Lena jumped up and shouted, Franklin stuck his hand out a little too quickly and they both ripped the wrapper off and had the first bite in their mouths in two seconds.

"Heaven!" squealed Lena.

"Thank you! Thank you!" mumbled Franklin with crumbs around his mouth.

Hiker Ben sat back and smiled, along with the other animals who seemed quite amused with the enthusiasm.

As they finished up, Franklin said one more time, "Man! That was good!"

"Glad it hit the spot."

After the animals had a chance to ask questions and Ben told his story again of how Boris, Bernadette, and others had saved his life, Franklin said, "Ben, we have made our home in a cave not far from here. Do you want to spend the night in there with us?"

"That sounds great! Thank you. I have a tent in my pack, but that would save me a little work."

"Perfect," said Lena, realizing she felt completely safe with this stranger. It was a very different feeling from the one she had with the stranger who had picked them up in his car. Plus, she knew Koda, Slash, and several others would rip him to bits if he tried to hurt them.

Pockie was watching and listening, and after the decision was made to sleep in the cave, he hopped up on Ben's leg and looked up at him with those deep, sweet eyes. Ben reached out and stroked his back. "Hey little buddy. What's your name again?"

"Pockie." He was a chipmunk of few words, but lots of affection. He closed his eyes as Ben continued to rub his head and back, talking to him in a soft voice.

Franklin and Lena were starting to really like this guy and felt badly they had lied to him about their names, but they didn't know what else to do.

The sun was getting lower in the sky when Ben suggested they walk to the cave, prepare some food, and then set up another bed for him to sleep in. Approaching the cave, they were feeling pleased to show him their little habitat. Lena knew it was swept out, mural to show off, food was organized, beds were fluffed.... "Uh oh," the thought suddenly hit her that the photograph of them with their parents was prominently displayed on a large boulder and if Ben saw that they wanted to see pictures of their parents, the story of them being abusive wouldn't make sense.

She ran ahead saying that she wanted to check something first. Franklin had no idea what she was doing, but had learned to trust her more than ever lately, so he didn't ask what she was checking. She had just tucked it away into their backpack when the guys arrived.

"This is a great place, Jake, and Hannah! I'm really impressed," announced Ben. "I will sleep like a baby tonight!" As Ben set his backpack down and began to unload it, the twins marveled at all the equipment he had. There was a little stove, fuel for it, a lighter, pan, cup, snack food, dried food, clothes, it went on and on and reminded them of Mary Poppins' bottomless bag.

"Wow!" was the limit of their language for a while and the only thing that kept falling out of their gaping mouths.

Ben said, "This is how you hike when you're prepared. I am very impressed with how you two have survived without any of this. I don't think I would have made it."

"We would probably be dead if it weren't for these amazing animals," Franklin confided.

"Well, what do you say we use some of this equipment?" asked Ben.

"I'm hungry!" "Sounds great!" they said simultaneously, another definite twin moment.

Ben set up his stove, Lena went to get water, and Franklin enjoyed resting from the fire making as the dinner packages were opened, prepared, and shared. They told stories about their experiences with the animals as they ate the freeze- dried beef stew.

The twins savored every bite, thanking Ben over and over.

Ben noticed their clothes were baggy and assumed that they had lost some weight with the new and sparse diet, but he didn't want to draw attention to it so he adjusted his question. "How long have you two been out here anyway?"

They had intended to keep a calendar but had been so preoccupied with the work of surviving each day that they had lost track and weren't sure what to tell him. Franklin finally offered, "We came to the wilderness on May fourteenth. What day is it now?"

"May fourteenth?" Ben was amazed. "It's August fourth. It's incredible that you've been able to stay out here this long. For several reasons."

The twins looked at each other. They shook their heads back and forth feeling both surprised at how much time had passed and proud that they had survived all they had been through. Ben began to look quizzically at them. "Aren't your parents looking for you?" he asked. "Probably not. Remember, they hate us," Lena said. "We may live out here forever," she added.

They noticed that Ben dropped the subject quickly, which brought them great relief. Neither sibling liked lying, plus, they really liked this Hiker Ben. He had bragged about the third pile of leaf and straw Lena had prepared for him while he and Franklin had been making dinner.

As they drifted off to rest with satisfied bellies, soothed by the sound of hooting owls and the song of the forest crickets, Lena asked, "Ben, what would you have slept on if you hadn't found us?"

"Oh, just a lame sleeping bag or my hammock," he answered.

Chapter 18

The Revelation

The next day was filled with more shared stories, Cubby, right at Franklin's side all day. Ben loved the sight of the quiet little bear who looked up at Franklin constantly and followed his every move. "Do you two spend time like this every day?" Ben wondered.

"Most days, but sometimes his mama wants him to stay close when I'm further out, looking for food or firewood," Franklin explained.

As they talked, Ben was fascinated by the way this "Jake" would sit on a log, mindlessly sketching pictures in the dirt; then, Cubby would duplicate his pictures with amazing precision. Clearly, these two kids had learned the animals far better than he had in his much shorter stay with them before. It was mostly the guys talking, but Lena would pop in from time to time. They were both happier than they realized they would be to connect with another human again.

Ben told them stories of his adventurous life and the more questions they asked, the more they unfolded. He had hiked the Appalachian Trail with a buddy before his experience there. He had rock climbed in Yosemite, surfed off the North Shore in Hawaii, on and on went the stories. The twins sat in awe of this cool, bearded mystery man and they found themselves relating to his love of nature and adventure.

Before Franklin realized what he was saying, he admitted, "I guess we can't stay here forever if we want to do some of these cool things, Lena." Oh no! He had just let two unintended thoughts slip out. "Uh, I mean..." He cleared his throat quickly. "Hannah. Lena is her middle name and sometimes I call her that." Franklin was sweating and biting his lip. He had gotten so lost in the adventures and so swept up by the idea of trying those same adventures one day that he may have made a big mistake. Lena just froze and Ben looked at him, just for a second, out of the side of his eyes. They still didn't want him to know their names when he went home because of who he might tell.

In the dead silence that followed, Ben shifted the conversation to the food. He wanted to hear all about what they had been eating. They were relieved, happy to have the topic shift, and energetically told him about all the plants as well as the regular meals of trout they had, thanks to the generous and skilled fishers, Wrigley, and Slash.

Lena bragged on her brother, telling Ben all about the grizzly encounter again and how he had endured so much pain while his leg healed, but never complained.

Ben shook his head and said, "I can't even imagine it. It's a miracle you survived that. I'm serious. I would have been crying for my mommy." They all chuckled. "If infection had set in..."

Lena couldn't resist interrupting, "It *did* get infected! You should have seen the pus!" She told the healing phase of the story in great detail, including the scrubbing, the forest medicines, having to wash all the blood out of his jeans, and getting him up and walking again. All of these things left Ben very impressed with each of them.

Later that evening, after playing with Cubby and Pockie and touring more of the area, Ben asked if the twins would mind showing him how they had cooked their fish. They were excited to give Slash an assignment, gather firewood and other materials, and set to work, showing Ben how to start a fire without a lighter, use sheep wool to catch the kindling on fire and build it, carefully, into a blazing glory.

Ben shook his head and smiled. "I hope my kids will learn to be as resourceful as you two," he said.

This filled Franklin and Lena with a sense of pride and a warmth in their chests they hadn't felt in a while. It also made them miss their parents very badly. Lena teared up but turned her head before Ben could see.

When Franklin asked, Ben told them about his wife, the kind and fun girl he had met in college. They had a ten-year-old daughter, Aspen, and an eight-year-old son named Bennett. He told them about all the activities his kids were involved in and how the whole family loved the outdoors like he did. As he talked about them, the twins could see how much he loved his family and how proud he was of them.

"I bet your whole family is great," predicted Franklin.

"Yeah, no complaints," said Ben. "I'm sad about my brother, though." When the twins looked at him, simultaneously, he added, "Long story."

After being further impressed with the way the twins skewered their fish for cooking to avoid dealing with the bones, he was excited to pull out a little pouch from his bottomless backpack and proudly announced, "Salt!" With a huge grin that showcased those white teeth and twinkly eyes, he reminded them of how much salt brings out the flavor of things. "I bet you guys are tired of bland food by now!" He handed the pouch to the twins to sprinkle on their fish and then generously dashed his own.

Even though they were anxious to try it again, the siblings were surprised at how strong the salt tasted to them. Their reflexes almost made them choke, but they disguised their reaction to keep from disappointing Ben. They whispered to each other later about how their taste buds must have changed and how they had both gagged. This gave them a little privately shared laugh when Ben had stepped away to put his salt gift back where it belonged. They thanked him, though. He, in turn, thanked them for the delicious meal, and they settled in for another night.

The next day, after breakfast, Ben announced that it was Thursday and that he would have to leave soon to get back to work by Monday. Franklin began to quiz him about when he had left home and how far they were from his home.

Ben told him that he had left Saturday morning and had hiked and searched until he found them on Tuesday. He figured they were about a day's hike to the nearest road. He would go through his routine of recharging his phone from a pocket charger and call his wife, Julie, to come get him. She would drive him to his car where he usually started his hikes. She knew the drill and was always very happy and relieved to see him return safely.

Franklin thought to himself how nice it would be someday to have a wife like Ben's.

Both he and Lena were suddenly sad listening to him review his plans. They had gotten used to the hiker being there. His company was comforting and fun. They loved their animal friends, but they had to admit something was special about this new connection. When he finished telling them his plans, he said, "Guys, can you sit down a minute? I'd like to talk to you about something."

"Sure, Ben," they both said in unison.

They looked at him with wide eyes and intense curiosity, wondering what was coming. They found him very interesting and predicted they'd hear another amazing adventure story. What he said, though, was "I think I have figured out something incredible. Something I never imagined when I left home." He paused and then went on. "The most I'd hoped for has happened; I found the animals again, and it's been a dream come true. You know?" He smiled at the twins while they wiggled in their seated positions and were nodding with understanding.

Lena interjected, "I can only imagine."

Ben continued. "The thing is... I think I may have found more than that."

Now, the twins tilted their heads, furrowed their brows, and looked confused. "Really?", asked Franklin, "What?"

Ben began slowly. "Many years ago, I stopped talking to my only brother over something so stupid. So stupid!" He looked down at the ground and shook his head. "I wanted to start my business, and I asked him if I could borrow some money. He loaned me a pretty big sum and, as my business grew, I paid it back little by...." He stopped and waved his hand at the still air. "None of that matters now. The long and short of it is that there was a disagreement, probably just a misunderstanding, about the money and we got mad at each other. We stopped talking. It was so hard. And now..." Ben looked up at the sky and choked up. After a minute of collecting his emotions, he finished. "And now there's no chance of ever talking to him again."

It made the twins choke when they saw tears in Ben's eyes. "Why? Why not?" Franklin asked.

Lena had already figured out his answer.

"He's dead. He was killed recently."

At this point, the twins got a sick feeling in the pits of their stomachs. They weren't sure what was going on, but the air felt so thick it was hard to breathe it.

Ben gathered himself and went on, "No matter who you two are, I think you're the greatest kids I've ever met - except my own, of course." Now a wink and a smile took over his face, which brought some relief in the middle of the rising tension. "But... I happen to think you're my family," Ben said, as thoughts and confusion were buzzing around in the twins' heads like a swarm of provoked wasps. He gave them a minute and then kept going, "I don't think you're Jake and Hannah. I think you're Franklin and Lena, my nephew and niece."

There was dead silence. The guilty-looking twins turned to each other, and, in a moment of panic, Lena spoke up, "Who is that? What are you talking about?"

"Stop it, Lena," Franklin interrupted. "She's normally not a liar. Don't tell me you're our Uncle Benjamin!" Franklin asked in disbelief.

"I am," the hiker said. The three of them sat and stared at each other for a while. It seemed like each one was waiting to see who would make the next move.

Ben spoke first, "I am so, so sorry about your parents. I can't even imagine what you two have been feeling and it's hard to believe all you've done, even though I've seen some of it with my own eyes. You are survivors, very courageous, and full of solid character. The animals have told me many impressive stories about what you have done here."

He noticed that the twins were completely silent and looking like they were still in shock. "I don't know what your dad has told you about me, but I promise, I'm not a bad guy." The twins vigorously shook their heads side to side but remained mute. "Grownups can make stupid mistakes just like kids and it was just a silly thing between us that we were too proud to fix. Anyway, there's no way I'm letting the State get you two. I want to take you home and adopt you. My family will love you guys."

Franklin and Lena were nearly knocked over. It took them a while before they could speak. Franklin was wondering what move to make so that they would be safest, and Lena was wondering how to apologize for all the lies.

Lena led the way. "I can't believe you're our Uncle Benjamin. Wow. And I can't believe you think we're good when we lied to you about who we were. I'm sorry."

"You were being smart and protecting yourselves. I don't consider that normal lying. You're forgiven."

Franklin joined in, having collected his thoughts. "You would adopt us? We won't go back if anyone tries to separate us. What did you mean when you said, 'the State?'"

"You two would absolutely stay together if you came with me. I can't imagine separating you," insisted Ben, and then added, "I meant going to an orphanage or a foster home."

Franklin relaxed. The air loosened along with their muscles and the three began to talk about what possibilities lay ahead of them. The twins began to feel excitement rising in their bellies and floating up into their chests.

Lena finally got up the nerve to ask, "What are your kids like? I mean, you told us what they like to do and all, but what kind of... do you think they would like us?"

Ben shifted and leaned forward toward Lena. "Absolutely! They will be so excited to meet the cousins they have only heard about. I saw you two when you were babies. We were all so happy for you guys. Twins! The only ones we knew of in the family and so cute! That was before the disagreement. That was the last time I saw you and I've wondered so many times what you were like. Now I know, and I think you will fit in very well with my family. My wife, Julie, is amazing. She will treat you like her own kids. I just know it."

So many thoughts were reeling through the twins' minds. The thought of leaving this wonderland and this magical experience with the animals was almost unimaginable, yet they were beginning to miss some of the things that they were used to in their life before. "Let us talk about it, okay?" Franklin asked Ben.

"Sure," he said. "We would have one more day with the animals and then have to head back or Julie will worry if she doesn't hear from me on time."

"Okay," Franklin responded, and the twins stepped away to consider the shocking news and offer that had just been dropped on them.

They talked and thought. Thought and talked. Franklin was asking questions like: What would it be like living with a family they didn't know? What would their school be like? Yet they already were pretty crazy about Ben. They didn't want him to leave. Lena's responses were: We may not have a choice. Police might find us any day and if they do, we will have to live with people we don't know anyway. They went on for a while and then remembered where they could get some advice that would take some of the pressure off them. Ursula. They would go see Ursula.

Chapter 19

The Decision

They were so happy and relieved when Ursula invited them to sit with her. Again, they were comforted by her presence and felt at ease sharing all they had learned and the decisions they had to make. The kind, grandmotherly bear listened patiently and then asked, “Did you think you would live here forever?”

Silence. Then the twins actually felt a little silly. They loved it in the forest with their new friends and never imagined life without them recently, but they also knew they were costing those same animals time, energy, and maybe even their safety.

“Where do you think you are meant to live, when you think about your futures?” she asked next.

The things they knew deep down to be true started to surface. They admitted that it didn’t make sense to stay there and grow up without any humans. They couldn't learn all they wanted to know, see other parts of the world, or enjoy the things they were able to do before. Franklin missed his real art supplies and playing ball with his buddies. Lena admitted she missed acting, dancing, and singing with friends. Ursula smiled and just nodded as these confessions were made.

"It looks like you have already made up your minds," Ursula finally announced.

"Hmmm, I guess we have," admitted Lena and Franklin, nodding in agreement.

"Thank you again, Ursula. You have been so good to us, and we will always remember the things you have taught us," Franklin said.

Ursula smiled and nodded. "Most of what I did was just help you recognize what you already knew," she said.

Lena asked, "Are we doing a good job of balancing our emotions with our logic on this, Ursula?"

"I surely believe you are," the bear affirmed with a pleased smile.

After they told Ben they had decided to go with him, they set about spending time with all the animals they had grown to love so much. Mitchie was the first one they decided to tell. It was hard to get the words out, because they realized that it might be hard for them to find these animals, just like it had been for Ben, if they were able to come back in the future. A few generations of chipmunks had come and gone since Ben was there last. It was a realization that made them both very sad. They were already dealing with the loss of their parents and now, the animals who had helped them survive and deal with their loss, may be lost to them too. But they decided together, with great determination, that they would return next summer and visit. No doubt about it. They just had to hope that they could find it and that everyone would still be there.

Mitchie sat across from them and listened for a bit. "Don't worry," he said. "We already know. We hear everything that goes on in these woods and things get communicated quickly. I knew this day would come. We all did, except for maybe Pockie and Cubby. They're young enough that it may take a little explaining. I'll let you decide whether you want to do that or let us take care of it.

"Listen to me. You two were sent to us for a reason. You are among the trusted. We have loved every minute of having you here and I hope we have helped you enough that you can go back to your world and have a long, great life."

Franklin interrupted. He was almost in tears, "Mitchie, you're the best friend anyone could imagine, and you have saved us, basically. I think we might be dead if it weren't for you and the others. If there's any way to repay you, just say it and we'll do it."

Mitchie continued, "You have given us more than you know, Franklin. You saved Cubby from the ghost grizzly, but mostly, your company has been great for us all. There's nothing for you to do except to keep the secret like Ben has all these years. It will be tempting to tell friends, and you will want to use it to feel powerful when people don't treat you well. If you do, though, our lives would be over. Everyone would want to capture us and make money off of us..."

Franklin and Lena both interrupted him, "No! No! No!" Franklin insisted, "We will never give you away. We promise!"

"I believe that to be true," said Mitchie. "That's what being 'the trusted' is all about."

The twins were determined to protect these animals at all costs.

They talked and talked some more about the memories they had made there as other animals began to join the circle that was forming. Ben appeared, after being gone a while. He sat with them too and told stories of his time there twenty years earlier. As he shared his memories with the mesmerized audience, Franklin noticed Cubby waddling up and scooting in beside him. Franklin wondered how much he had figured out but only reached over to pat him on the back. He remained quiet, listening to the stories and names neither of them recognized. Then, Pockie appeared and climbed onto Lena's lap. They sat there until it was time to go to bed. No words were spoken, but the twins felt their little buddies were sensing that something was changing.

When they got back to the cave, Lena pulled out the photograph she had been hiding. "Well, here's the proof," she said, presenting the evidence to Ben. He took it and held it a long while just staring and looking deep in thought.

Lena ended the silence by observing, "If you lost that beard, I think you might look a lot like Dad, actually." She winked at him and made him smile.

"Nah! I'm much better looking," he responded. The three laughed a hardy laugh that eased the tension of all the decisions for a moment and allowed them to relax into a deep sleep.

Ben sprang up first with the sun, but the twins followed shortly after. It was Friday, and Ben reminded them that this would be their last day. He knew they had to leave bright and early the next morning in order to get to a place where he could get cell service to call Julie in time.

Franklin and Lena had fallen asleep, planning what they wanted to do with their remaining time. Pockie had stopped sleeping in the cave when Ben came. They weren't sure why, other than his shyness, but Lena decided to find him first and try to explain what was coming. Franklin had decided to do the same thing with Cubby. Ben just wanted to talk to the animals as much as he could with the time he had left. This trip had not been anything like what he had expected.

When Franklin reached Cubby's usual hangout, he saw him drawing in the dirt. It made him wonder if Cubby would continue doing this after he was gone. When he got close, he could see what Cubby was drawing, and it surprised him. Cubby didn't look up but kept tracing in the dirt. It was an entire scene. There were trees, the stream, Cubby in the foreground, and a tiny figure that seemed to be Franklin far in the distance. Maybe he already knew.

"Cubby," he started, "There's something I need to tell you."

"I know," volunteered Cubby. "When the hiker first came, I knew this was gonna happen. I'm gonna miss you, but I think it's the right thing." Cubby paused. This was probably the most words Franklin had ever heard him string together at one time and they left him speechless. Cubby continued, "I wouldn't want to live with only humans, so I guess you wouldn't want to live with only animals."

Franklin jumped in, "I thought I did. I really thought I did... because of animals like you."

Cubby finally looked up at Franklin. He leaned against Franklin's leg as he often did and got the head scratch he often got.

"This is your best work yet, Cubby," Franklin said, pointing at the ground.

"Thanks. It's my saddest, too."

"Is that me leaving?" Franklin asked.

Cubby nodded.

"You are a true, melancholy artist, Cubby," Franklin acknowledged while he silently pictured this cub filling Koda's shoes one day. Cubby wasn't sure what melancholy meant, but it somehow made him feel understood.

Franklin invited him to tag along all day as he visited for the last time with the other animals that had come to mean so much to him. Lena had told Pockie, too, and asked him to ride on her shoulder as she went about her day. They expressed appreciation to Wrigley and Slash for all the fish.

Slash was surprisingly shy about being thanked. Franklin spent extra time with him, thanking the brave, somewhat clumsy and loveable, but heroic bear for saving his life. Slash had only looked down while Franklin spoke.

They told Henna and Nutalia that they had made a big difference with all the help they had given them, and the two chipmunks burrowed into the twins' hands for affectionate rubbing. Bellus came out to remind Lena which plant had kept her hair shiny, Fergus came to say goodbye and expressed some serious thoughts about how they had brought a new perspective to the community. He wasn't telling any jokes this time and they saw him in a new and interesting light.

As the day went on, the twins took turns spending time with different friends all around the place they had become so familiar with. They thought, surely, they would never forget what this place was like.

The next morning came before they were prepared. As they got up from their leafy beds, Lena thought about how she would miss sleeping in them. It hadn't been great at first, but now, she loved the peculiar crunch and earthy smell she buried herself in each night.

At first, her plan was to pull the leaves all out of the cave and toss them around, making it look more like it had when they had first arrived, but after a little more thought, she decided to leave them for the bears who would hibernate there in the coming months.

She packed their few things into the backpack and served the remainder of their stored food for breakfast. Even though Ben had come well-stocked, he was running low on food after sharing with the twins. He decided to ration what he had left for the trip back.

Chapter 20

Farewell Until Later

When they stepped out of the cave together, there was quite a sight to behold. From close to the cave entrance, stretching out as far as they could see in the direction they would travel, were furry and feathered bodies of all sizes, waiting to see them off. It brought tears to Lena's eyes immediately, but Franklin tried to hold back the ones he felt that were building up from wherever tears come from. He looked down at the lineup and then up to Ben who had unmistakable tears already in his eyes. That was all it took, and Franklin's began to fall from his eyes and down his cheeks.

At the head of the line were Koda and Ursula. They knew these two would always be immense figures in their lives. The twins hugged them but held on extra-long to Ursula. They had so much they felt the need to say, but words didn't seem enough, so they hugged in silence. When they looked up to her face, her expression reassured them that there was no need to speak.

Then, they moved on, offering their goodbyes to Slash, Wrigley, Bart, Scoot, Cubby, Luna, Spanky, Hannie, and the other bears. Next were the elk, Buck, and his herd. The twins were amazed at how much bigger the calves were getting. They were very steady on their feet now and twice the size they had been when they first met.

Following the elk were Banga and his mountain lion family, then, the longhorn sheep, Ramsey, Spook, Flibbity, and some younger sheep. When they made their way to the end of the line, there were, finally, the chipmunks. Henna, Nutalia, Bellus, Fergus, Ferbie, Rustle, their children, and Pockie.

Franklin reached down to scratch Pockie one more time and, finally, Mitchie.

Mitchie said, “I’ll be watching through the trees for you next spring. For now, it’s just farewell until later.”

“Exactly!” the twins said in unison. Twin moment.

Ben agreed. “Now that I have found this place, I don’t think I’ll lose it again.”

They walked, waving at the crowd until the trees finally blocked the last of the unforgettable little faces. This was hard. The twins had already been through more than most people can imagine, but this was really hard. The three walked in silence for at least a mile before anyone spoke.

Lena finally broke the silence with a question. “Did the animals make a line for you when you left before, Ben?”

“No. They were in a group, but they did all come to see me off. It was different, though,” Ben answered. That seemed to satisfy Lena because she didn’t probe any further.

“And we can’t tell a living soul,” she realized out loud.

“I know,” responded Ben with a solemn nod.

Thankfully, Ben had brought collapsible water bottles, and they had filled them full before they left the stream. They walked and walked for miles. Ben kept pulling out his compass and adjusting their direction slightly.

Franklin said, “It makes me feel better with you looking like you know what you’re doing.”

“We’re good,” Ben responded.

Lena said, “Don’t forget, he’s the one who couldn’t find that place for twenty years.” The guys chuckled at that thought. Then Ben asked, “Since you guys are trusting me with your lives anyway, how would you feel about calling me Uncle Ben?”

"I was wanting to call you that already," Franklin said.

"It's cool with me," Lena added. Then she asked, as they were tramping over broken tree limbs, "Dad called you Uncle Benjamin. Did you used to go by Benjamin?"

"Yeah, our mom never stopped calling me that, but when I got older, my friends started calling me Ben and it kinda stuck. People in the family are the only ones who called me Benjamin after that," he explained. "So, I guess you guys could call me Uncle Ben or Uncle Benjamin, whichever you like," Ben offered.

Franklin decided, "Well, we have called you Ben since we met you, so I kinda like Uncle Ben."

"Me too," said Lena. "Uncle Ben it is!" exclaimed Ben with a satisfied smile.

They walked until the sun was overhead and then stopped for a break and some food. While they snacked, they talked about all the food they had eaten. Most of it was pretty amazing. In fact, they didn't taste anything they hated except one thing... "Elk milk!" the twins exclaimed together. Ben spat out his water and almost choked. "What?" he asked, laughing, and looking at them like they were crazy.

Lena explained that Buck thought it would be good for them and that they would like it. "I don't know how they got it from the cows, and I don't think I want to know, but one of the bears brought it to us in our bowl one day so we were a little excited to try it. What we didn't expect was that it wouldn't be cold. You know? Isn't milk always cold?" They all laughed. "Well, not if it's straight out of a mammal," she continued. "I tried it first and gagged, but I didn't tell Franklin. I gave it to him, and he tried it, but spit his out."

"You're evil!" Franklin laughed.

Uncle Ben was laughing so hard now he couldn't catch his breath until he finally asked, "Did you tell them what you thought?"

"Oh no!" Lena said. "We didn't want to hurt their feelings. But after that, whenever we got tired of eating dandelion leaves, we'd just say to ourselves, 'better than elk milk' and crack up."

They continued their hike with occasional breaks. Uncle Ben checked Franklin's feet from time to time because his sneakers were so worn out they were starting to come apart. He wanted to make sure Franklin wasn't getting sores or blisters.

Uncle Ben told them about the town he and his family lived in. He described it as not too small but not too large. He told them about the school they would go to and what activities they could try. He told them many stories about their dad as a boy. They loved hearing some familiar ones told from a different perspective and also ones they had never heard before.

When the sun had descended to a low spot on the horizon, the twins got to see their Uncle Ben's pup tent for the first time. Franklin helped him set it up, but it was quick and easy. The twins slept in the tent on the opened sleeping bag, which made a fluffy quilt when it was zipped open and flattened. Ben strung his hammock between two nearby trees and slept there, trusting nature through the night.

The next day, after they packed up and were on their way again, Franklin started asking more questions about keeping the animals' secret. At one point he said, "I've been thinking. I used to want to be a veterinarian when I was little, but then I found out about the shots, the surgeries and all the things they do that scare animals, so I changed my mind. But now, I'm thinking that I can talk to them and explain what's going to happen and it might help them to be less scared."

"Hmmm," Ben thought for a minute. "But you know they may never talk to you."

"Yeah, I've been thinking about that too," Franklin added. "But it wouldn't matter. I would know they really understand."

Ben answered with, "Well, then, I think that's a great idea." He noticed Franklin smiling after that.

A couple of silent minutes passed, and the guys heard Lena, several feet behind them, mumble into the forest air, "I'm thinking medicine too, only people medicine. I think I might be cut out to work in a hospital."

They hiked and hiked, but both siblings noticed they had more energy this time. When they discussed it, they decided it was either that they had more food this time, they were in better condition this time, or maybe they had more hope this time.

With each step, they found themselves thinking less and less about the animals they had left behind and were thinking more and more about this mysterious Aunt Julie and the cousins they would be meeting soon. Uncle Ben had told them that it was a good thing they had gotten used to eating healthy nature food because their Aunt Julie liked to cook healthy food and didn't keep junk food around. She did have a habit of making cookies on Saturdays though. Just the thought of warm cookies made their mouths water.

After they had stopped for lunch and rested a bit, Uncle Ben had charged his phone and tried to get a phone signal. In no time, they heard the first electronic sounds they had heard in a long time. There was a soft, muffled ring that was carried through the clear air and then a voice.

"Ben! You're back! I can't wait to see you, just tell me where." Then it was his turn, "Julie, you're not going to believe this, but I have the best possible news..." He winked at the twins as he stood up and walked away for a minute.

They could hear most of what he was saying but tried to give him the privacy they thought he might want by talking to each other. They scrambled around picking up the food, packing, and prattling on and on about anything to make noise. They wanted to hear the conversation, but since Uncle Ben had walked away, they resisted the temptation to eavesdrop on whatever it was he was choosing to say to explain them to his wife. And then, they couldn't help but hear him say, "I know! I know!" because it was so loud. He sounded excited, so they hoped it had gone well. "Okay, we'll see you there! I love you so much!"

He had been walking back in their direction at the end of the conversation so that when he hung up, he was face to face with the twins. They were frozen still and completely silent in anticipation when their Uncle Ben shouted, with the excited animation of a kid, "You're in! I told ya!" He had a huge grin on his face and gave them big hugs. They clung to him for a while and then, took off with added energy, Uncle Ben leading the way.

Sore feet and tired legs were not even noticed now. It didn't seem like they had walked much farther when a road opened up in front of them. Civilization. They walked down the two-lane road until they made a turn onto a busier one. Cars flew by and seemed so fast. It was almost a weird experience to see cars again and they seemed so loud. As soon as they turned the last corner, Uncle Ben shouted, "There she is!" He pointed to a blue Jeep sitting in the parking lot of a small grocery store in the distance.

A woman jumped out and started waving. She had a big smile that brightened as they got closer. Franklin squeezed Lena's hand and said, "I think we're gonna be all right."

"Yeah," she agreed. "I guess we're out of the woods now."

www.ingramcontent.com/pod-product-compliance
Lightning Source LLC
LaVergne TN
LVHW091052080826
845145LV00002B/721

* 9 7 8 1 9 6 1 2 8 1 0 2 8 *